LEMOOR LIBRARY
ERS ROAD
OOR, WEYMOUTH

112350

2 0 AUG 2

The Case of the Deceiving Don

A SEAN SEAN MYSTERY

THE CASE OF THE DECEIVING DON

CARL BROOKINS

FIVE STAR
A part of Gale, Cengage Learning

DORSET COUNTY COUNCIL		
Bertrams	22.01.09	
	£17.99	

GE Learning™
aven, Conn • Waterville, Maine • London

GALE
CENGAGE Learning˜

Copyright © 2008 by C. W. Brookins.
A Sean Sean Mystery.
Five Star Publishing, a part of Gale, Cengage Learning.

ALL RIGHTS RESERVED
This novel is a work of fiction. Names, characters, places and incidents are either the product of the author's imagination, or, if real, used fictitiously.
No part of this work covered by the copyright herein may be reproduced, transmitted, stored, or used in any form or by any means graphic, electronic, or mechanical, including but not limited to photocopying, recording, scanning, digitizing, taping, Web distribution, information networks, or information storage and retrieval systems, except as permitted under Section 107 or 108 of the 1976 United States Copyright Act, without the prior written permission of the publisher.
The publisher bears no responsibility for the quality of information provided through author or third-party Web sites and does not have any control over, nor assume any responsibility for, information contained in these sites. Providing these sites should not be construed as an endorsement or approval by the publisher of these organizations or of the positions they may take on various issues.
Set in 11 pt. Plantin.
Printed on permanent paper.

LIBRARY OF CONGRESS CATALOGING-IN-PUBLICATION DATA

Brookins, Carl.
    The case of the deceiving Don / Carl Brookins. — 1st ed.
      p. cm.
    ISBN-13: 978-1-59414-677-0 (alk. paper)
    ISBN-10: 1-59414-677-2 (alk. paper)
     1. Private investigators—Fiction. 2. Minnesota—Fiction. I. Title.
  PS3602.R643C36 2008
  813'.6—dc22   2008016372

First Edition. First Printing: August 2008.
Published in 2008 in conjunction with Tekno Books and Ed Gorman.

Printed in the United States of America
1 2 3 4 5 6 7 12 11 10 09 08

We meet many people on our journeys on this Earth. It is inevitable that we lose some along the way. January 2007 was memorable for me in that I, and many others, lost two Barbaras. Both were writers, friends, and special people. This book is dedicated to them and to their memories: Barbara Saranella and Barbara Stuhler.

ACKNOWLEDGMENTS

Sean Sean lives and works in the Twin Cities of Minnesota, a vibrant, exciting and sometimes very cold place to be. He owes his existence and his adventures to many people who helped along the way. Among them are the dedicated members of the Roseville Police Department, my wife Jean, my keen-eyed writer's group, Anne, Tim, Mary Monica, Michael, Joan, Susan, Julie, Scott, Kent, and the best author's touring group ever, Ellen Hart and Kent Krueger, The Minnesota Crime Wave. And of course to Richard Prather. Special thanks to Gordon, John and Tiffany. This is a work of fiction. Liberties were taken with some of the geography and character traits to serve the story.

CHAPTER 1

The day changed dramatically when I turned off County D onto my short street in the northern Twin Cities' suburb of Roseville. Half-way down the single block, just about opposite my driveway, two squads were stopped in the street, red and blue lights flashing in the late afternoon sun. There was a small crowd of people on the lawn in front of the newish redwood sided rambler across from my home.

I slid my foot off the accelerator and idled on down the street. I couldn't quite reach my driveway. The Roseville officer standing by the open driver's-side door of her squad looked over her shoulder at me and made a pushing movement with one hand. I recognized her, although I didn't remember her name. She'd shown up last summer at the block party some of the neighbors throw every year. The idea of the party was to get to know people living in our immediate neighborhood. It was a good idea.

This was no block party. The officer came over to me. "Oh, hi, Mr. Sean. I'll move so you can get in." She knew where I lived.

"What's going on?" I asked, squinting into the sun.

She ignored my question and moved the squad car a little closer to the opposite curb so I could get by. I swung left into my driveway and parked. Now I could see what everyone was looking at. By the opposite curb directly across the street lay the wreckage of what appeared to be a wheelchair. In my suburban neighborhood wheelchairs are almost as ubiquitous as automobiles.

There are four retirement homes within a five-block area in my neighborhood. Three of them used to be public schools. Seemed to me an appropriate adaptive use. In the spring and summer the older folks living in the homes, those who can and who have such vehicles, can often be seen tootling up and down the paved pathways and streets, especially when the weather is nice. A few of them get an outing when relatives come by to push them around the streets. Others have battery-powered wheelchairs so they're more independent.

"What happened?" I said again, stepping out of my tired gray Taurus.

"Some old guy got killed," muttered a teenager wearing a reversed baseball cap on his close-cropped head.

"Killed? Car hit him?" Even as I heard the words come out of my mouth I knew that couldn't be right. There were dark marks on the pavement and curb that might be scorch marks. The frame and two wheels of a shiny black wheelchair stood on the street at the curb, but the seat and upper part of the device appeared to be missing. One of the wheels in the street was bent. I could see that this particular wheelchair had been one that was powered by a big battery. The battery case was wrecked, its top bulged upwards. There was no civilian vehicle nearby. Looking more closely I noticed that other pieces of the chair, including the seat and arm rests were scattered on the lawn of my neighbor across the street. There was a blanket-covered mound on the lawn.

I saw a Roseville Police sergeant, one I knew from previous contacts, standing in the open door of the other squad. She rested one arm on top of the vehicle. Her collar insignia winked in the sunlight. The small group of people standing around was quiet, subdued. It was as if they couldn't believe whatever it was that had happened here in a quiet neighborhood of a peaceful suburb called Roseville. I didn't believe it either and I still wasn't sure exactly what it was that had happened.

I walked into the street toward the nearest squad until Sergeant Lasker noticed the movement and looked over. When she recognized me she shook her head and flicked well-manicured fingers at me.

"What's happening, Sergeant?" I asked.

"We're waiting for the ambulance and crime scene people to get here." Just then her radio squawked. Sergeant Lasker turned her head slightly and spoke into her mike. "Right. Come in the other way. Over by the home. Take Luther Drive."

There was an answering squawk. We all heard the ambulance approach when it was a couple of blocks away, and then, as it came closer, the siren dying. It was clear from the passive stance of the cops and bystanders there wasn't any hurry. If it was a person under the brown blanket on the lawn of the house across the street, he, or she, was long past any need for haste.

The ambulance pulled into my neighbor's driveway and reversed into the street so the rear was close to the blanket-covered mound. The emergency techs did their thing and loaded the body onto a gurney and then into the ambulance. The driver consulted briefly with Sergeant Lasker out of my hearing, and they drove off. Ms. Lasker—I didn't know if she was married—returned to my side of her car.

She shook her head. "Man was running himself up the street here. There was an explosion that blew apart the wheelchair and killed the old man instantly."

"Some kind of malfunction in the battery?"

"No, although that's a reasonable guess."

"What then?"

"We won't have a definitive answer until the crime scene guys do their thing. But there was a peculiar smell when I arrived.

Also bits and pieces."

"Such as?"

"Broken window over there." She waved at the house directly across from mine. "Largish explosion. Too big for a malfunctioning battery. But not huge. I think the window blowout is a fluke. Also I see stuff that doesn't look like it ought to be attached to one of these wheelchairs."

"Bomb?" I asked. "You must be kidding. Who's the victim?"

She consulted her notebook. "Unknown at the moment. No ID on the vic. An officer is talking to the staff at the home over there." She nodded at the nearest retirement home, a former junior high school a block away. "We'll canvass the neighborhood in a little while, find out if anybody saw anything."

I glanced around again, fixing the scene in my memory and turned back to my own driveway. That's when I noticed the silver-blue Audi down the block toward Brenner. To this day I still don't know why that vehicle registered in my consciousness. Maybe 'cause I didn't think I'd seen it in the neighborhood before. Being a private detective, I'm trained to notice things that are even slightly out of the ordinary. The late-model Audi was parked just below the small hill that connected my street and Brenner. It was too far away to hear the engine, but I had a feeling it was running and that one or two people were sitting inside watching. I couldn't be sure, and I wasn't going to walk down there to check it out, was I?

I went up my steps and unlocked my front door. While I disabled the alarm system, the cats demonstrated their delight at my homecoming by rolling on the carpet and displaying their rounded bellies. I touched the shotgun bracketed over the door inside the front closet. I don't know why I do that. I guess it's just a habit to reassure myself it's still there, ready if I need it. I've noticed some guys have a habit of touching their fly occasionally. I touch my shotgun.

The Case of the Deceiving Don

It had been a frustrating, boring and hot day, sitting in my parked car watching some clown who had a whopping claim for a job-related injury. The insurance company had heard the guy hadn't been as badly injured as he claimed. Apparently they also had some question about the ethics of the guy's doctor. So instead of paying the claim right away, the insurance company hired me to follow and observe. They wanted pictures of the claimant doing something they could take to court to disprove said claimant's back injury. So far, I hadn't seen anything useful.

I grabbed a beer out of the refrigerator and uncapped it. Took a long pull that disposed of about half the contents. Sitting in a car for six hours in the heat isn't my idea of fun. I can't run the air conditioner because I have to start the engine and that calls attention, which I don't need. When I'd decided to become a P.I., after the cops said I was too short, none of the P.I.s I talked with mentioned how tedious surveillance gigs are, or that they are a large part of the biz. On the other hand, the death of the old guy in the wheelchair put my surveillance discomfort into perspective.

I slid open the deck door at the back of the house and went outside. I settled into my favorite chair and stared at the back lawn. The mosquitoes weren't too bad yet, but the lawn needed mowing. I sipped more beer and thought about the sudden violent death of a man I had never met. I also considered whether I was up for running the mower.

The doorbell chimed.

Chapter 2

I unlatched the door and twisted the knob. I don't have a security chain on my front door. I probably should. I should probably look to see who rings before throwing wide the door in welcome. I don't do that either. I do have a steel-core door in a heavy steel frame, however. I opened the door.

On the other side of the screen stood a uniformed officer with a notebook in her hand and a slight smile on her lips. In my professional life as a private investigator I try to have good relations with the cops, but I didn't know this officer.

"Good afternoon, sir," she said. "I'm sorry to bother you but we've had an incident across the street, and I need to ask you a few questions."

An incident. Right. "Sure," I said. "Do you want to come in?" I opened the door wider and heard, in the background, a pulsing siren as a patrol car rushed along Fairview, probably in pursuit of a speeder, or maybe on an emergency call to one of the retirement homes in the neighborhood.

She came on in, and we sat down in the living room. Officer Wang Ping quickly established my stats, and I showed her my identification. We also established that I couldn't tell her precisely where I'd been just before the explosion that had sent the old guy to his reward.

"I was somewhere on the freeway, 35W, approaching Johnson Parkway, I guess, coming from my job in Saint Louis Park."

"Were you alone?"

"Alone."

"Where were you working today?"

"Sorry, officer. I can't tell you that. Privileged, you see. But it was way across town."

She nodded her dark head and made a note. "What did you see when you arrived home?"

I told her in as much detail as I could remember. Then I said, "There was an Audi."

"Sir?"

"An Audi parked on the left hand side of the street—that would be the east side, just up from where it joins Brenner. The engine was running and there were two men in the vehicle. They were watching the scene." I hadn't been sure about all that until I said it. Something told me there were two men in the car and they weren't just passing time at the curb.

Officer Wang Ping frowned and made another note.

"Ask the EMTs. They drove past the car. Twice. It was a silver-blue late model Audi."

She had a few more questions, then she thanked me and left. I closed the door and went to the phone. I called Catherine Mckerney. She's my lady love, a tall, willowy massage therapist and school executive. She lives in the upscale Kenwood area of Minneapolis, and she's very important in my life. She wasn't home, so I left a message and went back out the front door.

The cops had tied a bunch of yellow ribbon around the big oak tree across the street. They'd stretched it out to stakes and a squad at the curb. I walked closer, and the cop on duty got out of his car. I waved and stopped, hands on hips, looking at the scene. The overhanging branch of the old oak tree had a lot of singed and blackened leaves on it. My neighbor's almost perfect lawn had a couple of brown burned spots close to the curb. I stared at the spots for a couple of moments and then pivoted slowly to my left, unobtrusively scanning the houses and street in the immediate vicinity. The silver-blue Audi was gone. Crime Scene techs were all over the place.

Once I detected there wasn't much to be seen at the scene, I went back inside and down to the basement where I cleaned my other shotgun and my gat. One of my gats. There was no particular need; they'd both been cleaned only a week ago, but I like the smell of gun oil and powder and the feel of the weapons. Always have. I don't carry a weapon even when I'm working, except occasionally. As a licensed private eye, my job sometimes requires it, but not often. Besides, carrying a hand gun and some ammo weighs me down and ruins the lines of whatever I'm wearing. It's permissible in Minnesota, where I live, to carry a concealed weapon. Or an unconcealed one. It would be hard to discreetly follow someone with a holstered weapon hanging from your armpit in plain sight. In Minnesota summers, the few men going about the streets wearing suits or coats appear to have something to hide. Usually.

I'm not a cowboy, so most of the time I go about my daily work un-weaponed. It's never been a problem. So far.

I sat in my basement smoothing oil on the surfaces of the shotgun and running the cleaning rag up and down the barrel. I was enjoying myself. There's something sensual about handling and caring for a good quality weapon. I hadn't planned on cleaning my shotgun, or the other weapons in my small arsenal, but it seemed like a good idea. I was still unsettled from the explosion that killed that old guy, even though I didn't know him. What gave me a minor chill though was the Audi, the one parked a block away with somebody in it just watching. The men in the car could have had a perfectly legitimate reason for being there. In that particular place, at that particular time. But I didn't believe it.

After awhile I went upstairs and called Catherine again. She still wasn't in. I mixed myself a gin and tonic and watched the

The Case of the Deceiving Don

evening news. Mostly it was the usual stuff. They hadn't yet reported the death on my street. I thought that was a little unusual, but maybe it happened too close to deadline.

I went outside and sat on my front stoop to watch a few dog walkers and joggers and other neighbors sauntering by. No TV news teams had shown up. Maybe they were finally getting tired of chasing accidents. Of course this death hadn't been an accident. If it was a bomb. A few passersby waved; others just checked out my gardens and thick tangle of ferns that protect me from having to spend lots of time mowing grass. I sat and wondered who the old guy was and why anybody would want to blow him up. Another siren. That made three so far today. This one a speeding ambulance, lights flashing, that zipped up Fairview, a block over. Not an uncommon occurrence in my neighborhood, given the retirement homes nearby.

After it got dark, I went inside to get away from the mosquitoes. At a quarter to ten, the telephone rang for the first time since I got home.

"Sean here," I said

"Mckerney here," came a familiar voice in her often amused tone. "I detect you are home," she said.

"How was your day?"

"It was productive, busy. All in all a good one. Yours?"

We hadn't been together for a couple of days. Although we are a tight couple, our lives are very busy and take us in different directions, so it is sometimes several days between direct contacts. I began to notice that even when I was working on a case that took me out at odd hours, I missed Catherine more and more if I didn't see and smell her, she of very subtle perfumes. I told her about the death of the old guy right across my street.

"That's terrible. What an awful way to go."

"True, but I understand he was very old, had been a resident of the home for a long time and died quickly. I talked with an Officer Wang who came by canvassing the neighborhood. She said the cops were of the opinion he felt nothing."

"Well, I hope so. Did you know him?"

"Nope. There is one thing though," I said.

"Unh oh."

Catherine had a well-honed instinct about me. The tone of my voice seemed to give her hidden messages.

"They didn't tell me his name, and I don't know any of the people who live in that place. I offered a guess that somehow his battery in his electric wheelchair had exploded. Overheated maybe. The cop in charge didn't exactly disagree with me. The one thing is this. A block away there was a car with one or maybe two guys in it. They were just watching."

"Oh dear."

"What?"

"Oh dear, I said. Signs and portents. Is that car really significant?" Catherine asked. She sometimes accused me of finding or manufacturing reasons to get involved in cases. I maintain it's just my regular old curiosity.

"Yeah, it just gave me an odd feeling. Why is this car with two guys just idling at the curb? They don't get out; they don't roll down the window. They're just there. And then, after a while, they aren't there." We talked some more and made a date for lunch later in the week. " 'Bye, love," I said.

"Back atcha," she responded, and we broke the connection.

While I looked through my mail and stared out the window, a sedan cruised slowly by. There is no streetlight on my block. Naturally I couldn't see who was in the car, and it was too dark to see the color or the make, but I had my suspicions. Boy, did I.

Chapter 3

The next morning I went to my City Hall at Lexington and Country Road C. It's not my personal city hall, you understand. It's the one in Roseville, the city where I live. It was difficult. We voted in a bond issue last fall after a certain amount of wrangling and construction was under way. The construction resulted in blocked off lanes, closed parking areas, detoured traffic clogging nearby streets, a lot of dust, noise and general pandemonium. Inadequate signage. Nevertheless, I was patient and I persevered, two of my better traits, according to Catherine.

I finally found a parking space, and wonder of wonders, there inside, in the police department, was my contact in this city, Sergeant Helen Lasker. She came to the reception area and buzzed me into the sanctum.

When we were settled in her tiny office I said, "Do you get a bigger cubicle when the new place is finished?"

She shrugged and shifted in her chair. The belt with all her gear on it creaked. Helen Lasker made her small office look even smaller. She was an imposing chunk of woman. Taller than average. I put her at a little over six feet. She wasn't fat by any measure. Thick brown hair braided intricately around her well-shaped head and a voice that made you pay attention when she talked. "I guess so. To tell the truth, I haven't asked."

"You lose a lot of time going back and forth to usher someone through the security door."

Helen nodded. "Rules. Ever since nine-eleven, you know. I'm

fine, my dad is fine, you look fine. I assume Catherine is also fine. Enough with the small talk. What brings you here this fine morning?" She grinned at me.

"Yesterday's incident."

"Sean, are you making a formal inquiry here? Got a client?"

I shook my head. "Nope, and no. I just want to know what's going on in my neighborhood, on my street. I got the message yesterday that wheelchair malfunction wasn't the cause of the deceased becoming so. Am I right?"

"Yep. We don't have all the lab reports back yet, but at the moment, we're investigating this death as a homicide."

"Ah. Have you identified the deceased yet?"

"Sure, that was the easy part." She picked up a form off her desk and scanned it. "The deceased is a white male, eighty-seven years of age, in reasonable health, considering. His name is Augustus Molinaro. He was a resident of the Lakeland Homes, aka Sheltering Limbs, and had been for fifteen years. He lived with a younger man who was his paid attendant. He died as a result of a small explosion. CS guys think an explosive was wired to his wheelchair battery which powered the detonator."

"Do we know how it was triggered?"

"Not yet, but we will," said Helen in a firm voice. "It's not even twenty-four hours."

"I'm cool. What about the Audi?"

Her eyebrows went up. "What Audi?"

"I told an officer after you left. Silver-blue, late model Audi. It was parked about a block down the street, east curb, just up from where the road curves into Brenner."

She shook her head. "Not in the file. Maybe the officer hasn't reported in yet, although . . ." Her voice trailed off. She looked at the file and shuffled a piece of paper.

"It might be nothing. Car was parked facing north, toward us, with the motor running. My impression was two guys in it.

Probably not significant."

Helen Lasker stared at me for a moment. "But you don't think it was nothing, do you?"

I shrugged. I do that sometimes. "Not sure. For not being able to see anyone through the windshield, I just have this impression the two guys were watching the action with other than the kind of curiosity you get from people at fires and accidents. You know. Like they didn't get out of their car to get closer or ask what was going on. Obviously I haven't any facts here."

"Yeah. I get the distinction. I'll check it out. Anything else?"

"Nope. Thanks for your time."

Lasker got up and trailed me out to the security door and saw me through. I went into the heat of the day and walked to my car. Across the crowded lot, I saw the tail end of what looked like a silver-blue automobile going away down the exit road to the street. I couldn't tell what kind it was.

I drove through the rising heat to my small office in a medium-sized office building near Northeast Minneapolis. It's on Central Avenue, which is no longer central to much of anything important. I guess it was at one time, but the city grew in different directions. Except for my office. The mail had already been delivered so I sat at my old wooden desk and went through it. Most of it was the kind of mail anybody gets. It didn't meet my low threshold of interest and usefulness, so it went directly to the wastebasket. There were a couple of bills and even a check for service rendered. The check, a sizeable one, was from one of my major clients, Harcourt, Saint Martin, Saint Martin, Bryce *et cetera*—they had about a million associates listed on the letterhead. Harcourt, Saint Martin, Bryce was one of the premier law firms in the state. And they paid well. And on time, which is important to small business entrepreneurs like myself.

I'm a private investigator. A short private investigator. What I do is poke around in people's business, often it is business said people don't want me poking into. And the people I'm poking at are occasionally not very nice. So there's sometimes an element of danger. Or excitement. And once in a while I have to call the cops about a client. Those clients frequently don't honor their commitment to me. That's understandable, I guess, but it doesn't get my rent paid.

So I'm always happy to see a fat check from a client. I made out a deposit slip and endorsed the check. About then the telephone rang.

It was Helen Lasker, from the Roseville Police.

"CS guys report that an explosive charge was in fact wired to the battery. It may have been triggered by an odometer."

"A what?"

"An odometer. You know, that's a thing that measures distances."

"Yeah, like on your car. So an odometer was connected to the wheelchair and that made the contact?"

"Right."

"Boy, that's callous. What if he'd been in the dining room of the residence or in some crowd when it went off?"

"I know."

"Okay. Thanks for the update. Anything else?"

"No, but I'll try to keep you in the loop. Since you're such an *interested bystander*."

"Thanks. I owe you," I said and set down the telephone. I got the message in her voice. I'd ignore the message.

The outer door opened, and a large man entered. He was followed by a second large man. They were wearing white shirts, tasteful ties, and dark suits that looked expensive. The first man walked over and sat in the client chair facing my desk. The other large man looked around, and when he didn't find a second chair, leaned against the wall between my safe and my old coat rack. The other office chair was out for repairs because a would-be client broke the back in anger. He was irked because I refused to take his case. It involved trying to find evidence that his wife was cheating on him. I never take divorce cases. At least, I don't unless the cash account is empty. He got mad and threw the chair across the room. I wasn't sure what he thought that would accomplish. I already knew he'd beat on his wife on at least one occasion. After I threw him out of my office I never saw him again.

I stared obliquely at the two large men in my office and thought about saying something by way of greeting. I chose not to. They appeared to be giving me the Intimidation 101 routine. It wasn't going to work. I took my eyes away. I didn't want to make them nervous. On the other hand, I wanted to be sure I'd recognize these two the next time I encountered them. So I looked askance. The silence stretched on, and finally I got tired of waiting. I was ready to go to lunch.

"How can I help you gentlemen?" I always like to start with a positive assumption.

Large Number One, he in the chair, said, "We want to hire you."

"Okay," I said. "What for?"

"We checked you out. You've got a good rep. In your line."

"Okay," I said again. "I don't do divorce work, I don't kill people for money, and I avoid illegal activities whenever possible. What do you want me for?"

"What's your fee?"

"That depends."

Large Number One shifted his weight to the other buttock. The chair creaked. So far, Large Number Two hadn't said anything and hadn't moved from his place against the wall. I was pretty sure he was breathing. "Depends on what?"

"On the degree of risk. I have kind of a sliding scale. I know, Philip Marlowe didn't work that way . . ." I paused long enough that it appeared they'd never heard of Philip Marlowe, "but I do. My base rate is $75 dollars an hour plus expenses. All expenses are extra, including any trips to the emergency room." I smiled briefly. It was a small joke that went unappreciated. "You get a detailed list of activities and other expenses. Payments are to be kept current." I was sounding like a corporate bookkeeper.

"Okay," said Large Number One. "A friend of ours was killed yesterday. We want to know who did it."

I don't believe in coincidence. "Is this about Augustus Molinaro?" I said.

Chapter 4

After my large visitors, now clients, left, I added their large bills—they paid a retainer in cash—to my deposit envelope and hied myself first to my bank in Saint Paul, and then to the Muffuletta across the street from the bank for a nice Cobb salad. While I ate, I cogitated—that's a word I learned somewhere—on my latest clients. They were probably connected, as in Organized Crime, the mob, Mafia, whatever terms you want to apply. I had my suspicions. Except that they were a walking cliché. They looked as if they'd been watching all the movies about OC, or maybe the Teflon Don, John Gotti, was their hero. Which is why I distrusted my reaction to the pair. I figured I'd have to do some research.

In the old days, as explained in my detective manuals, the ones written by people like Kenneth Millar and Elizabeth Linnington, the cop or the P.I. beat the old shoe leather, talked to a lot of people, asked a lot of questions; followed leads wherever they took him. That led ultimately to an answer, a solution to the puzzle, in this case who killed Gus Molinaro and why. I live in a somewhat different world, as do we all. It's a world of faxes, cell phones, computers, and the Internet. I would whip back to my office and let my fingers get calluses, instead of my bunions.

I turned left out of the restaurant and walked up the street under the broad canopy of leafy branches of the elm trees along the boulevard. These big old elms had survived various diseases and urban abuses. I glanced up the street and noticed a late model Audi going slowly up the hill away from me. I thought about that and realized I might be getting paranoid. More probably it was that odd experience many of us have upon buying a new car. We think we have chosen an unusual model or a rare color, only to stumble across many similar vehicles after our purchase. Not being a psychologist, I have no idea what this condition is called, or if it even has a name. Do I care? Not a lot. Except that my powers of observation are important to me in such circumstances as I now found myself. I had the feeling that somebody or something was watching me. Possibly it was just my natural paranoia. But the dead man was much in my thoughts.

There were a couple of workable scenarios. I assumed that the dead guy had some influence or some importance at one time. Otherwise my large clients would not be paying for an independent investigation. They would have kicked back and let the local police agencies do their thing. It could be they just generally didn't appreciate or trust the cops. Lots of people are like that. Such an attitude brings me business. The other thing that helps keep me clothed and fed is the number of people who don't want cops messing about in their private affairs. It could be that my two clients were worried that the cops would find something. Something like information my new clients didn't want revealed.

The second scenario was one I didn't like and hoped was not the case. It was possible my clients were looking for the perpetrator of the hit on Mr. Molinaro because they wanted to hit him, or them, back. A matter of macho pride, you see. Assuming the death of Mr. Molinaro was a hit. If it was a hit, I had to assume there might be a connection to the mob, the mafia, Organized Crime. Them. It was a depressing idea. So far in my career I'd managed to avoid such entanglements, mainly because I liked my life and didn't trust anyone hanging around that group. I feel the same about gangbangers. I intend to live a long life, so besides staying away from those thugs, I don't do drugs, I don't drink to excess, I tend to eat regular. My body is a temple, yada yada yada. Right.

My new clients had appeared at a time when I could use the money and when I was irked by a killing practically on my doorstep. Mostly I'd managed to keep my professional life away from my personal life. I wanted it to stay that way. I'd already half decided that I was going to assist the cops' investigation if I could, since it was now pretty clear the death of the old guy was murder.

My two new large clients hadn't been very forthcoming. No phone. They gave me an address which I happened to know was a remailer, a place where you can send mail and have them resend it to a different address. If you were very circumspect, that second address might be another remailer and so on for as many steps as you wanted to use to feed your need for privacy or your paranoia. It cost money, but that usually didn't matter much to those who used such services.

What I couldn't yet decipher from my conversation with the Large Ones was their relationship to the deceased, Augustus Molinaro. Friend or Foe? That indeed was the question. I needed some background on the deceased. A little old-fashioned detecting was in order. I'd apologize to my bunions later.

I drove back to my favorite suburb, parked in my own driveway and walked around the corner to the Sheltering Limbs retirement and assisted living establishment. The one where the late Mr. Molinaro had been living when he departed this earth.

As I went along the sidewalk to the main door I passed their parking lot, scanned it for silver-blue late-model Audis, and sauntered inside. At the reception desk I encountered a sweet-faced, rather plump woman of indeterminate years who asked me my business.

"I'm assisting the authorities in the inquiry into the unfortunate death of a former resident, Mr. Molinaro. Gus Molinaro."

"You a cop?" she asked.

"Private," I said. "Can I talk to Molinaro's companion, attendant, or whatever you call him?"

"Sorry, no." She didn't sound the least bit sorry.

"No? Is he otherwise engaged?"

"Sorry, Mr. Levy is gone."

She didn't sound the least bit sorry about that, either.

"Gone? As in decamped, skedaddled, in the wind?"

She nodded. "He came back right after the . . . accident, packed his belongings and was gone in less than an hour. Left a mess in his room, too."

"This happened when?"

"Early last evening."

"Do you have any information on him? If he was an employee—"

"He wasn't."

"No?"

"No," Sweet-Face asserted. "He was personally employed by Mr. Molinaro. I know because there were a few problems about that."

She was about to go on, but a man appeared beside us who turned out to be the director of the facility. He was a tall, stork-like man who introduced himself as Director Tompkins, "Harry Tompkins, pleased to make your acquaintance, isn't it a nice day, and what can I do for you?" I had no reason to doubt the truthfulness of his statements, so I shook Mr. Tompkins's hand and let him lead me down the tiled hall to his office. He sauntered on long legs. I sort of trotted to keep up.

His office walls and ceiling were painted institutional beige. The curtains on the half-open windows were bright yellow and so was the vinyl covered couch that faced his desk. When the breeze fluttered the curtains, it was almost like there was a fire in the window. There was a row of tan file cabinets—all locked, I noted, against one wall, and two other chairs. I took one of the chairs, a hard-back office chair with a pale blue cushion on the seat.

"How may we be of assistance?" Harry Tompkins, Director, said. No hand-rubbing, no obsequiousness, just a straightforward question. Well, we'd see.

"I'm Sean Sean," I said, offering a business card. "I'm making some inquiries."

Tompkins's eyebrows went up while he read the lettering on the card. "A private investigator. My my. This is rather unusual. I can't recall the last time we had a private investigator here asking questions."

"I'm making inquiries into the background of one of your guests"—I almost said inmates—"a Mr. Augustus Molinaro. I'd like a little background. Whatever you can provide." I smiled and spread my hands. I can do obsequious.

Tompkins frowned. "Really, Mr. . . . Sean. I'd like to help you, I really would, but I'm not at liberty to talk about our guests here at the residence. We pride ourselves on maintaining absolute privacy for our guests. You understand, I'm sure."

I think he was gearing up to deliver a much longer speech, but I held up a hand to cut him off at the pass. "Surely, Mr. Tompkins, since Mr. Molinaro is now deceased, there'd be no harm."

Tompkins shrugged. "I'm really very sorry."

"So there's nothing you can tell me such as when Mr. Molinaro came, about his family or anything of that nature?"

Tompkins nodded and shrugged again. "I'm sorry, absolute discretion is our rule. I'm just not at liberty to say anything at all about Mr. Molinaro, or about any of our other guests. I'm sure you understand. In fact, I'm not at liberty to tell you whether Mr. Molinaro is, or was, a guest here at Lakeland Homes."

"Yes, I appreciate your situation, Mr. Tompkins. And your discretion."

So I asked him some general question about the owners of the place. How long had he been there—he wouldn't say; what was the cost for a private room—he'd get me a brochure; what were the credentials of the staff—more paperwork.

"All right, that's helpful, Mr. Tompkins. I have just a couple more questions."

Tompkins folded his hands and looked at me expectantly.

Chapter 5

"Let's chat about a certain Martin Levy."

Tompkins frowned. "Mr. Levy was not an employee. I doubt I can tell you very much about him."

"I'm aware that he didn't work for you. He lived here as a personal attendant to Mr. Molinaro. Correct?"

"He worked exclusively for Mr.—one of our guests," Tompkins responded.

"Of course. How old is the man, would you say?"

"Oh, I never really thought about it. Younger than I am, certainly. He appeared to be in very good shape. I suppose he was around thirty or so. Perhaps a bit older."

"I see." I made a note in the notebook I carry for such purposes. I don't like to rely too heavily on my memory in these interviews. I never understood how Mike Hammer and Philip Marlowe retained so much in their minds. "Could you describe him in a little more detail, please."

Tompkins frowned in thought. "Well, as I say, he's about thirty, with dark curly hair. Dark brown, I think. He wore it short. Overall he was quite acceptably groomed. And, as I say, he kept himself in good shape. I know he frequently used the exercise room here. He once told me he had a membership at a local health club, Lifetime Fitness or something. He wanted access to more strenuous workout routines. He wore tight tee-shirts with cropped sleeves much of the time."

"Muscle shirts," I murmured. "He was an attendant to one

of your guests for a long time, I take it?"

"Oh yes. He came with the individual he attended about five years before I arrived to take over as director. So that'd be fifteen years."

"Uh huh. Any distinguishing marks that you recall?"

Tompkins thought for a moment then he nodded. "He had a small scar high up on his right cheekbone. Sort of a moon or crescent shaped thing. I think he'd had some kind of accident because the fingers on his left hand appeared misshapen. I believe they sometimes caused him a little discomfort."

"Can you be a little more specific about the injury?"

Tompkins thought for a moment. I didn't try to prod him. "Two of his fingers are curved, or bent. The third and fourth fingers, I seem to recall. They might even be fused together somehow."

"Was he right or left handed?"

"Oh, he was right-handed. He was about six feet tall, and he probably weighed around one-eighty or so."

"Anything else that stands out, Mr. Tompkins?"

"His accent. He was from somewhere out East although I couldn't say exactly where. I'm not good with regional accents. But Mr. Levy certainly didn't sound like a Midwesterner."

"Any other distinguishing marks?"

"Well, he has a tattoo."

"A tattoo?" I said.

"Yes, he has a tattoo of some kind of bird on his . . ." Tompkins hesitated and then touched himself on the left arm. "Yes, on the left side. It ran from his upper arm, you know, from his bicep, from just below the shoulder, down over the inner arm to his wrist. Quite elaborate it was."

"Do you recall what kind of bird?"

"No, not really. It might have been a peacock or a bird of paradise, but he never said specifically."

"And you never asked, I take it?"

Tompkins looked at me without responding. Then he nodded once. "That's right. I never asked."

"How would you characterize his relationship with your client?"

Tompkins's gaze rose over my head to the ceiling. After a moment of silence during which I heard birds twittering in the small tree outside Tompkins's window, he said, "Interesting question. They never fought, you understand. But I don't think they were very friendly. I never heard him raise his voice to anyone. Mr. Levy tended promptly to his client's needs, and I never heard Mr.—er, his charge, complain about anything, so far as that goes, but there didn't seem to be any real connection between them. Mr. Levy was conscientious and he kept a watchful eye out, but it was a job, not a commitment."

I waited a moment, checked my notes and then said, "Thank you, Mr. Tompkins. You've been very helpful." I stood and offered my hand. Tompkins rose smoothly from his big chair and we shook hands again.

"You are quite welcome, Mr. . . . ah, Sean. I'm sorry I couldn't be more forthcoming about the late Mr. Molinaro. But I'm sure you understand. As I explained, we offer complete and absolute confidentiality."

I smiled and turned to leave, saying, "That's perfectly all right. I do understand." Jeeze Louise! I couldn't decide whether Tompkins was stupid or very smart. I concluded that it didn't matter, although I was pretty sure he thought he was playing me.

I went down the hall to the reception desk and asked the woman there for a member of the maintenance staff.

She smiled—sweetly—and told me how to get to the basement office of the maintenance staff. I went there.

It was a cheerless, concrete-block, windowless room, cluttered with brooms, shovels and racks of supplies. It smelled faintly of bleach and other cleaning solutions. Maintenance Engineer Willard Johnson was seated with his back to the open door and his booted feet up on his miniscule wooden desk. I rapped on the door frame, and he glanced back over his shoulder.

"Hiya," he said. "What can I do you for?" Unlike Mr. Tompkins, Johnson didn't get up.

I stepped inside and introduced myself.

"Huh," he said, shaking my hand. "I never met a private eye before. I bet you have an interesting life, doncha?"

"Sometimes," I acknowledged. "But often it's just boring."

"Well, have a seat if you can find something." He waved one hand at the room. I found an empty, upended, drywall compound bucket and sat.

Willard grinned and nodded. "So, you on a case or something? A private eye, huh. Cool. You carry a gun?"

"Yes and no." I smiled. "Guns are dangerous. I'm trying to get a little background on one of your fellow workers. Martin Levy?"

"Huh. He wasn't no fellow worker of mine. Not on the staff. Personal attendant he was. Came with Mr. Molinaro. One of our guests. Can't talk about him, you know. Privacy. It'd be my job if somebody was to find out I talked to you about Mr. Molinaro. Too bad about the old guy. I never had much to do with him, but he was always nice whenever we came across each other. 'Course he was never alone. That Levy guy was always there."

"I understand that Mr. Levy occasionally went to a health club. Mr. Molinaro must have been alone then, wasn't he?"

"Well, I suppose so, but I never saw him out of his room without there was Levy hanging around. Even in the playroom, where they have games and such. Levy was always around, watchin'."

"Watching. What does that mean?"

"Well, it means that I thought he was paying attention to everything and especially everybody in the room. All the time. I remember one time, just last week it was. Molinaro asked for a glass of water or juice. One of the staff said she'd do it for Levy. He wouldn't let her. He did it himself. An' he always looked hard at everyone who came into the room. Anyway, I just got the feeling Levy was payin' attention to everyone."

"Talk to him very much?"

"Nope. That's another thing. No gossip, no chit chat. Not a friendly type at all."

A sly look came over Willard's face. "You want the lowdown on some guest, talk to the residents." He nodded. "Some of them know a lot."

"Thanks for your help," I said. I got up off the bucket and left Willard Johnson to his work break.

When I reached the main floor I was moving right along, my white soles sending little warbling songs into the silence. Rounding a corner I almost walked into a short, slender woman I took to be a nurse. She smiled at me and did a quick two-step to avoid a collision. I exited the institution and started on my way home. A quick scan showed no silver-blue Audis in the vicinity. I knew there was a health club down in the mall about a mile away. It stood to reason Levy would have gone someplace close so he wouldn't be away from his charge for very long. That was my next stop. I walked away from the building, intent on retrieving my car from my driveway.

Chapter 6

I walked around the building and started toward Brenner, which would take me to the foot of my street. A paved walking path circles Langton Lake behind the park that abuts the residence home property. The path goes around the swampland to the south between the houses and the trucking terminals off the freeway. It ends, or begins, at the corner of the retirement home's property where it meets the street. Some of the staff who still smoke take breaks along the path at the back, near the rear entrance where deliveries are made. There's a picnic table and bench there with a butt can. When I got to the path, I wasn't far from a tree I remembered well from the previous summer. I'd had an interesting late-night conversation with a man holding a gat on me beside that tree. This day there was a nurse, leaning against a different tree smoking and watching me. I took a chance and turned toward her.

"You're the one asking about Gus, aren't you?" she asked.

"Am I?"

"Yeah, about Gus. Mr. Molinaro." She nodded. "He always wanted us to call him Gus."

A faint chime pinged in my head. "Gus," I repeated. "Yes. I was asking. Did you know him, this Gus? Ms.—?"

She shrugged and stubbed out her cigarette in the rusty coffee can by her left foot. She wasn't going to tell me her name, and she wasn't wearing a name tag. "We aren't supposed to talk about the residents. But yeah, he was a nice guy. Friendly.

Whenever we were in the rec room, he would kid around with us. But there was something going on with him and that Martin Levy."

"What do you mean, going on?"

She tugged on her earlobe. My eyes were drawn to her gesture, and I saw that her earring was in the shape of a B.

"Well, whenever they were talking, it was always low, with their heads together, know what I mean? Like they had secrets." She paused, glanced around.

I nodded and shifted my weight to the other leg. Waited for her to continue. It's something I learned from my training. Waiting. I had to work for several years with an older, more experienced investigator before I got my license. I didn't find that in any of the detective books I read. In books you can't have a lot of pauses where nothing happens.

"When you even came close they'd stop talking and just look at you. After you went on by they'd start talking again."

"Did that happen often?"

She shrugged in what I took to be a non-committal way. "It's really sad what happened. I liked Gus, Mr. Molinaro."

I could see she was tearing up. "What can you tell me about his attendant? Martin Levy?"

"His jailer you mean."

"His jailer?"

"Yeah. Gus called him his keeper or his jailer. I don't know why. But Mr. Levy was always hanging around, you know? He was always there. Sometimes he'd say something like, 'we can't do that.' Or 'no, that isn't possible.' "

"But he wasn't with Mr. Molinaro—Gus—when the accident happened."

"No. It was right after they spent some time in the game room. I saw him wheeling down the main hall toward the front entrance."

"You mean Gus?"

"Yes, Gus."

"Where was Martin Levy?"

"I don't know. They left the room together. Then I had to go—I had to get something, so I went out and I saw Gus almost to the front door." She stopped and sniffed. Then she poked at her left eye with a crumpled tissue.

"Are you a nurse at this establishment?"

She looked at me out of her right eye. "Yes, I am."

When it was clear she wasn't going to say anything else I thanked her and said some meaningless words meant to comfort her. They probably didn't. Then I walked on along the street. There aren't any sidewalks in my neighborhood.

So, I thought. It was coincidental, wasn't it, that Levy would leave Molinaro alone just on the very afternoon his chariot was scheduled to go boom. Or maybe Levy planned it that way. Maybe Levy was getting intelligence from somewhere and things had changed, because fifteen years is a long time to dance attendance for a guy who isn't your brother or your pop and for whom you apparently don't have a great deal of affection. Curiouser and curiouser, as Alice once remarked.

I walked on home, alert to my surroundings. One of my neighbors was out mowing his lawn. Apparently he had the afternoon off. He gave me a friendly wave. Other than him, nobody besides me was on the street. I didn't see anything else even remotely suspicious, although I did hear another lawn mower motor off in the distance somewhere. The sun was hot and even the birds were quiet.

When I got to my house, I booted up my computer. I now have two, one at home and one at my office. I'm a little slow getting into the cyber age. I can type pretty well, so I use the computers mostly for note keeping and writing letters and bills. Especially bills to clients. When I want to do research, my first

The Case of the Deceiving Don

inclination is to go to the library or call one of my numerous contacts around town. But I'm becoming more familiar with the Internet as a research tool. My neighbors down the hall at my office are seriously into the whole computer biz. In fact, that *is* their business. They do programming and other kinds of computer stuff for their clients. The Revulon cousins, Belinda and Betsey, are my unofficial teachers, periodically helping me out and, at the same time, clueing me in to various tricks to make me more efficient with the technology. Sometimes I think they think they are my collective mother as well. I fished my pocket diary out and transferred some jottings to my computer.

BC, that's Before Computers, I pretty much filled my days and many evenings with work for my clients. And since my client list doesn't seem to grow, now I had more time on my hands to sit around cogitating. Or playing cards. Or drinking ginger ale.

If I was in a book, I'd spend the time in bars or with my main squeeze. Trouble is, my main squeeze, Catherine Mckerney, has a business of her own to run and couldn't spend hours and hours playing grabass with me—more's the pity.

I did a simple Internet search which didn't net me anything of interest. I emailed the Revulon cousins. I got an immediate response that they would do some complex searching for me. Ten minutes later, while I was in the kitchen making iced tea, the computer dinged to warn me I had incoming. It was from Belinda Revulon. Her Internet search had hit the jackpot.

Greasy Gus Molinaro was a made guy. He'd made his bones in the fifties when the Mustache Petes still ran most of the Mafia families. He was Sicilian and rose steadily through the ranks until he became an under-boss of some repute, at least on the East Coast. Here in the Midwest, we apparently never heard of him. Shortly after Bobby Kennedy rode into D.C., the wars happened between the government and the mobs and between themselves. Gus dropped out of sight during that era and was never heard from or about, again. It was assumed he had died or been snuffed. In either case he was out of the picture. Maybe he'd taken the old advice and come west.

Chapter 7

I called my friend Rick. Ricardo Simon is a first class homicide dick in Minneapolis. We occasionally help each other out. I try to remain on good terms with cops in both Minneapolis and Saint Paul, not to mention my own suburb. There are a lot of things the cops can accomplish that would be hard for me to do in a timely fashion. On the other hand there are certain things I can do they can't, without running afoul of something called the law. Ricardo wasn't in the office. I supposed he was out solving crime. I had his cell number, but I was reluctant to use it except in emergencies, so I left a message at his office and then I called Sergeant Lasker at the Roseville cop shop. She promised to make some inquiries and get back to me.

While I waited for return calls, I went to my basement workshop carrying one of my weapons. As I may have mentioned, I keep a slightly modified shotgun in a specially designed bracket in the closet above the front door. Just in case. I haven't needed it for some time, but I cleaned it and reloaded it, just in case.

Then I opened the safe in my basement and checked my arsenal. I don't have a lot of weapons. I rarely carry my favorite, a 1911 Colt .45 caliber semi-automatic. It's too heavy, and it costs a lot when I shoot it. Bullets aren't cheap. But when I need a serious weapon that gets respect when I draw it, that baby fills the bill. It's the same handgun the military issued to the army for a lot of years. If the slug hits you, it tends to take you out of the action. Instantly.

I'd just cleaned my .45 semi-auto yesterday, so I just looked at it and put it back in the safe. Then I went upstairs and made me a glass of iced tea. On my back deck, which looks out on a very small lawn fringed with many tall trees, bushes, a few hostas and other things that grow well in shade, I thought about Don Molinaro. Greasy Gus. I rested my head on the back of my chair and glanced up through the trees at the deep blue sky. If this was the same guy, what was he doing in a quiet retirement home in Minnesota? Maybe just what it looked like on the surface—retiring.

Now me, I'm a trained detective so I'm supposed to delve beneath the surface and try to get at the underlying, hidden, inner secret meanings of things, but I couldn't for the life of me figure out what he was doing here. Oh, I had a few wild fantasies. He was here to organize the Twin Cities. He was in the witness protection program. He had relatives here and he wanted to be near them. Right. Maybe his old girlfriend was in that same home. Nuts.

My neighbors, Dan and Maria, share with me a couple of large old cottonwood trees. The tree seeds, attached to those fuzzy white fronds that act like parasails, were all over the place. I saw a bunch, a whole squadron high up in the air, higher than my chimney, actually, sun glinting off the seed husks. They were just drifting quietly along, peaceful as could be, maybe a hundred feet up. It was nice. Then the telephone rang.

It was some clown selling wildcat oil-well speculations. He first wanted half a mil for a full share. I politely told him I didn't have that kind of moola to give him, so he scaled it back to a ten thousand dollar piece of a group share. I suggested in stronger terms that I wasn't interested and I needed the phone line. I told him to get off the line forthwith. He didn't, so I did. I hadn't even taken my hand off the instrument when it rang

The Case of the Deceiving Don

again. This time it was detective Ricardo Simon.

"Crider's Buns is outa business," he said somberly.

"You have got to be kidding. Half the force buys those goodies. And you, you live on those things."

"I know. It's a sad day around here. Your message said something about a dying don? I wish you'd use plain English, sometimes."

"Does the name Molinaro, Augustus Molinaro, mean anything to you?" Long pause. "I hear he likes to be called Gus."

"Hey! Yeah. Gus Molinaro! Greasy Gus. Name like that, he coulda been a Beaner like me."

"Ricardo—"

"Yeah yeah, I know. Molinaro, right. Sure. He was a small time capo somewhere out east. Mighta been New Jersey, or maybe Pennsylvania. Got eased out and absorbed into a bigger organization."

I understood Ricardo to mean that there had been a territorial dispute and when the dust cleared and the bodies were buried, Molinaro's people were either dead or integrated into a more powerful crime family. "Whatever happened to Molinaro?"

"That I'm not sure about," said Simon. "He disappeared, or left town, or was murdered. Maybe all three. I'd have to check. Boy, that's a blast from the past. I haven't heard that name in forever. Why, Sean? It can't be for your memoirs. He was a few years before your time."

"I think he may have been living here in my town for the last ten or fifteen years."

"You're kidding."

"See what you can dig up will you?"

"Well, if he was in the witness protection program, we might not know, probably wouldn't. If he was on his own, we probably wouldn't know unless he got up to his evil ways out here. How'd this come up on your radar?"

"If it's the same Molinaro, he got killed a couple of days ago almost in my driveway." I paused. "Blown up in my street, actually."

"Was he coming to see you?"

"No. Turns out he lived in the Sheltering Limbs retirement home over a block. When the weather was decent he apparently rolled around the neighborhood in his motorized wheelchair. The bomb blew him out of the chair when he was going by my place."

"Jeeze. Somebody wanted to make real sure, didn't they?" The line was quiet for a bit while we both thought about the abrupt death of a man we didn't even know. Then Simon went on, "I don't know if we have anything on him but I'll check and see, get back to you maybe tomorrow."

"Thanks, buddy." I hung up.

So, I mused, a former member of the mob has been living for ten plus years right here in our bucolic neighborhood. Verrry inntaresting, as Arte Johnson was fond of saying on that TV series a few years ago. Why? And why was he snuffed now? I was going on the assumption that something changed, or that new information had become available that made Gus's elimination an imminent requirement. Lots of questions.

I called Helen Lasker.

"Dammit, Sean, you think I got nothing to do but take care of your business? And furthermore, I don't know why you're involved in this anyway."

"Client, my dear. A paying client. Have you anything for me?"

"Yes," she said, "but mostly negative. No we didn't know an ex-mobster was living in Roseville. No, we didn't know his real identity. No, none of the state or federals that would talk to us had any information on the guy."

"Do you think they were forthcoming?"

"Generally, yes. Oh sure, some crap about need to know and homeland security from a couple of them. The FBI office, the CIA, the US Marshals and the Minnesota Department of Public Safety all denied any current knowledge of Mr. Molinaro or his whereabouts. They also expressed surprise at his recent address and even more recent demise."

"Legit surprise, you think?"

"Can't always tell, but yeah, in this case, I think so."

"Did you get anything from the Witness Protection people?"

Helen laughed gently and said, "Do I ever? Not that I have much truck with those people, but naturally they denied everything. According to the marshal I talked to, they didn't know anything. He wasn't even interested in why I was calling, so I didn't tell him Gus was a goner."

"I really appreciate the update. What do you think now?" I asked.

"Now I think we have an open case of homicide and between me, thee and the heather on the moor, Mr. Levy is our prime suspect. I'll appreciate anything you turn up."

"You and my clients will have my best efforts. Count on it." I softly hung up the telephone.

Chapter 8

I called my lady love, the tall, the elegant, the willowy Catherine Mckerney.

"This is Catherine." Her voice never failed to send shivers up my back. "Hello?"

"Hi, babe," I said, trying for low and sexy. I got a giggle in response.

"Sean, you're never gonna master it."

"You recognized me?"

Catherine produced a very unlady-like snort. "None of my other lovers try to pretend as hard as you do. Now if you had a French accent . . ."

I let that slide. All of it. "How about dinner out? I have a new client, and I'm feeling flush."

"Sounds excellent. And if you're a very good boy, maybe I'll give you a flush."

"I flush at the possibility," I responded. "Casual, I think, no tie. Too hot. I haven't chosen a place yet, but I'll pick you up about seven."

"Terrific. I can't wait," she giggled again at our games and clicked off.

At seven on the dot I arrived at Catherine's Kenwood area apartment. I walked into the elegant lobby and winked at the security camera. The electronic security lock buzzed raucously, and I went through. I was glad her building had pretty good security ever since we'd had a little dust-up with one of my more violent targets. That dust-up had put her in the hospital for a short while and had made me really mad. It also made me realize, if I needed reminding, of how important to me in my life, Catherine Mckerney had become.

Now see, that's worth knowing because most independent P.I.s eschew personal relationships. That's partly because of our attitudes toward life and its rules and mores and partly because of the kind of work we do. Let's face it; if the bad dudes you are up against know about your close personal friends and lovers, your loved ones might become targets. That's exactly what happened to Catherine. But I had fixed that, forthwith. I tried to be careful so her exposure was limited. Tonight, her exposure was of a different sort.

The elevator door slid open, dispelling my random thoughts like gossamer wisps of smoke in a wind storm. I sauntered down the long, well-carpeted hall to the first intersection and hung a left. The door at the end of the short hall was open, and my friend was standing there waiting. In her hand she held a glass of amber liquid and ice. How neat.

Catherine was wearing a long dress. It was dark red or burgundy with a subtle flower pattern. It had spaghetti straps that left her nice shoulders available to my eyes. I could see her bare toes peeking out from beneath the hem. The heavy tumbler she held was laden with ice and my favorite scotch. I knew that without touching it or smelling it because she often made me a drink when I arrived at her pad, her place. I'm a detective, after all, and I was familiar with the good brand of scotch she stocked.

Once she waited for me in the open door with a glass of scotch and ice and nothing else. That is to say she wasn't wearing any clothes. But not tonight. Tonight she was dressed to go to a nice but casual restaurant, in keeping with my own attire. I was wearing a light cream linen jacket over a crisp white short-sleeved shirt, open at the throat. My summer-weight slacks were dark grey. I'd showered, shaved, cleaned my fingernails; I was the bee's knees. We were a cute couple.

We went to a nice quiet restaurant called The Living Room. It was only a block from the Fine Line Cafe, right on the edge of the Minneapolis central warehouse district where a lot of the upscale and younger up-and-comers congregate for a night on the town. The Living Room is so named because it's decorated in the fashion your favorite ninety-year-old aunt might have chosen for her drawing room. Except the lighting was lower. The place had several rooms connected by wide arches, two fireplaces that had real fires when the weather was cold, several comfortable love-seats, and a couple of sofas, complete with fringes along the bottoms and elaborately carved dark wooden feet. There were carpets on the floors, and most rooms had intimate dining alcoves for two to four patrons. There was a larger, more efficient dining room as well, which was a lot more like other restaurants in that it had several tables. All the tables for meals had pristine white cloth covers. The restaurant used heavy plated silver cutlery and nice glass if not crystal. Patrons usually arrived early for their reservations in order to partake of a relaxing drink or two and intimate conversation. The sound system had cost a lot of money, and the owners didn't desecrate their investment with bad music. They played jazz—cool, tasteful, jazz from the forties and fifties interspersed with a little thirties stuff from the Duke and others. Benny Carter, Herbie Mann, Dave Carr, Stan Getz, early Brubeck. Like that.

The Living Room is a place where one goes to unwind, have a romantic interlude, a nice dinner and a pleasant experience. It also is a place where impatient people don't go. The kitchen is excellent but not to be hurried. That's why, after more than an hour of sipping scotch—Catherine shared my affection for good scotch—and conversation about our separate days, the rising

The Case of the Deceiving Don

sound of voices from the room behind us caught my attention. There was some kind of altercation stewing.

I snagged the passing waitress and said, "Excuse me, Patty, what's going on?" We knew her, you see, being long-time, if infrequent, customers.

Patty frowned prettily and leaned closer so we both could hear. "Out-of-towners, I think." She shrugged. "Your dinner is about fifteen minutes away." She went off on her rounds.

Catherine put a tempering hand over mine when I swiveled my head to look into the adjoining room. I couldn't see the source of the noise that continued to rise and fall. Other diners were starting to notice the unusual hubbub. I smiled at my companion and got to my feet.

"Don't worry, sweetie. I don't plan to interfere. Just a visit to the facility."

Catherine smiled and nodded. "Try not to hurt anybody."

Trouble was, I had to walk into the next room, source of the loud voices, in order to get to said facility. I strolled across the room, glancing at the table of four suits from which the row was rising. A waitress I didn't recognize was at their table, placing glasses on her tray. She was facing me, and her forced smile was apparent.

When I returned from the bathroom, very clean and pleasant smelling, by the way, Melvin Kartasian, one of the owners, was standing at the table. I'd done a small job for Mel a few years ago and we'd become casual friends as a result. Not all of my clients become friends. I try to be discriminating in the jobs I take on. It keeps me alive and out of the hospital—mostly. But I don't get palsy with all my clients, either.

As I passed, there was a sudden lurching movement at the table. One man lunged to his feet jerking his wrist away from the hand of his table companion.

"What tha' hell," he slurred. "We been waitin' almos' anour.

I wan' my dinner." He was pugnacious and surly and one of his companions was egging him on. I knew Mel could handle one guy, but two might be a problem.

I stepped up to the table. "Gentlemen," I smiled. "Is there a problem?" As I spoke I unbuttoned my coat. I wasn't carrying, but I had a fleeting thought of every other western movie I've ever seen in which somebody unbuttons something to make a hog leg easier to get out of the holster. It's a provocative gesture. The table reacted.

Now I'm not big. I'm not built like Shell Scott, or Pronzini's Nameless Detective. I'm five-one or five-two or so and on my good days I weight a mere one-thirty-five. Yes, I have worked hard and learned a few moves. But I didn't want to tackle this guy and throw him into another table. That would make a mess and be more trouble than he was worth. The boor making the noise leaned forward, favoring me with a contemptuous sneer and a load of bad breath. The other three were starting to shove their chairs back.

"No guns, Sean," Mel said sharply. He knew I wasn't carrying heat, but his words caused just enough hesitation in the three still seated to give me the extra edge I needed.

I put a hand up on the boor's shoulder, right above the muscle at the joint between shoulder and spine. There's a nerve. It's very sensitive. I squeezed. The effect was almost instantaneous. It hurt and his arm started to go numb. His eyes got wide and he leaned again. Backwards this time. I smiled and he fastened his gaze on my face. I have this game face I sometimes use. I practice it in front of the bathroom mirror. I don't think he liked what he saw. I pressed forward and the guy sat suddenly. I gave him just a little more squeeze for emphasis and said, very softly and distinctly, "Stop fucking around and be quiet. Please."

Then I let go. Boor, suddenly a bit more sober, grabbed his

shoulder and shook his head at the three other men at his table who were watching me warily. I nodded at Mel and walked slowly back to my table in the other room. On the way I intercepted a few covert glances from other patrons as if they thought they should know who I was. I tend to avoid public confrontations. One of my values as a private dick is my anonymity. If I'm good at my job, I don't get ink in the local press. I slide in, do the job and get out. No mess no fuss. And no headlines.

When I sat down at my table my lovely companion wrinkled her nose and sniffed. "Umm, I love the way you men smell after these confrontations."

I sipped my scotch and raised one eyebrow, something else I practice.

"Funky," she went on, "maybe it's the testosterone." I felt her bare foot slide up my calf. She grinned. "Makes me hot," she whispered.

Dinner arrived and we left that subject for later examination.

Chapter 9

The next day I was in my office doing routine things. It was boring. Opening neglected mail, throwing out trash, filing new bills, even endorsing checks. Today was a real bonanza. Two checks had arrived for recently completed jobs. I went down the hall to the mail drop. There was a window at the end of the building just beyond the mail slot. It gave me a nice view of the street through the recently cleaned glass. Central Avenue wasn't so neat and across the street was mostly tarred roofs of the buildings. Up the block on the other side, parked near a fire hydrant, was a late model ice-blue Audi.

Shit!

I dropped my letters, including the one to the bank, in the slot and stood to one side of the window close to the wall. I eyeballed the car for a few minutes. There wasn't any movement, and I couldn't tell if there was anybody in the vehicle. The light was wrong. Then I heard the elevator start up. So I waited some more, glancing from the window to the elevator doors behind me. The elevator stopped on second, one floor below me. Nothing else happened for a few minutes so I went back to my office.

I had just settled into my chair and slightly moved the box I keep under it for my feet when the door opened and two large gentlemen entered. My clients had returned.

"We've come for a report," said Buzz Cut, the man who had paid me the cash.

The Case of the Deceiving Don

"Why don't you sit down?" I offered.

"Just report," he said.

"Do you drive a late model Audi?" I asked. "Sort of an ice-blue color?"

The two guys blinked at me. "Why?"

I sighed. Getting information out of these guys, even with a rubber hose, would be a real chore, I figured. I didn't have any real evidence to back it up but I was pretty sure by now these two were mobbed up, but I'd been able to establish that they weren't the bombers. Probably.

"Just curious." I smiled my most winning smile. "It's only been two days, you know. Can't expect much in that time. I'm still compiling a list of people to question. Haven't had time to get all of Gus's background."

"Gus?" The man stared at me. His gaze was steady. I could imagine how that stare would look over the barrel of a blue-steel semi-automatic. I have a very active imagination.

"Yeah, Greasy Gus. More specifically, Don Augustus Molinaro, aka Gus, aka Greasy Gus. From Pennsylvania. Mechanicsburg, I believe." There wasn't the slightest reaction from the hard guy standing in front of me, but the other man grunted and shifted against the wall. It seemed to me it got a little hotter in my office right about then. Maybe the air conditioner had stopped working.

"I have to tell you, I have this rule about taking on clients from the mob, the Mafia, the black hand." No reaction. "You know, Organized Crime."

"Don't worry about it," said suit number one, Mr. Buzz Cut. The other one, the one against the wall, I'd dubbed Mr. Hands. He had the biggest hands I'd ever seen on a human being.

"Well," I started.

"There are exceptions to every rule. This is an exceptional situation. I paid you and I expect you to do the job."

"I could refund your money," I said.

"Unacceptable," responded Buzz Cut. "We'll be in touch. But I want a little more progress."

Buzz Cut, the less huge of the two and the one who seemed to be in charge, laid another C-note on the front edge of my desk. Then the two large hard guys turned and left without another word. I exhaled softly. The apparent temperature in the office dropped. When I heard the elevator start, I grabbed my Nikon out of the bottom desk drawer, jumped up and hurried down the hall to the window by the mail slot. Even with the telephoto, my view of the two gentlemen wasn't the best but I fired off three shots, catching them in high oblique profile through the window. When I lost sight of them, I checked the lot from my window.

The ice-blue Audi was gone.

I sat down again in my creaky wooden office chair. I was tired of explaining to the happy couple that it was difficult for me to deal with cash on the barrel-head, so to say, and No Name as a file folder label didn't fit very well. Since I wasn't making any discernable impression on my clients with my doubts, I decided to ignore my concerns and get on with the job they were paying me for. I also decided to check in with Sergeant Helen Lasker.

"Sean, what's up?" she said, coming on the line.

"About Augustus Molinaro, aka Gus, aka Greasy Gus."

"Yes?"

I could tell I had her full attention. "He is or was a minor capo in some eastern Pennsylvania town called Mechanicsburg. So you probably have an organized rub-out on your hands," I said.

"Really. Thanks for nothing. Any thoughts on who the perp might be?" she asked.

"Not yet," I said, "but I agree that Martin Levy is a strong candidate. The real questions are why and why now?"

"Molinaro was in residence here for at least ten years and his minder, Levy, was here for the same number of years." Lasker coughed gently into the phone and cleared her throat. "Far as we know, Levy was a devoted companion. He was always there. Staff at the home assumed he was trying to be as protective and helpful as possible. The arrangement was unusual, a resident with a personal attendant.

"Even when Levy was off on his own, apparently a rare occasion, he stayed nearby. When he was at the gym, only a few blocks away, for example, he always called Molinaro sometime during the middle of his routine."

"Have you got the sequence nailed down on the day of the murder?"

"Yes, we're satisfied. A normal morning. They appeared for breakfast, then did the routine stuff. When the weather was nice they went outside. Unless it was hot or raining."

"Or a blizzard," I injected.

"They often went around the block once or twice, sometimes took that path at the back of the place into the park for a ways."

I heard her rustle some papers and then she went on. "Staff said they were going around the block as per usual except that it was a little later that afternoon. We've established that they went out the front door, across the parking lot and east along County Road D."

"Was that normal?"

"Hmmm. Lemme see." More paper rustling. "So we're told. Sometimes they went around the block the other way, but this time they went right on Mildred and were tooling down the street toward Brenner when the bomb went off. Got that from a witness who lives near the corner. She was setting out her sprinkler."

"So where was Levy?"

"Exactly. The wit recalls a man walking behind the chair, but that's the last we have. She couldn't say how far behind. There weren't any witnesses to the actual explosion, this one had just gone into the house. Leastways none we can find. It wasn't a huge bomb, so if Levy knew it was due to go off he wouldn't have had to be very far away."

"What persuades you Levy did the deed?" I asked.

"He's not here to question, is he? He didn't hang around. We have a witness or two who are pretty sure they saw him trotting down the hall at the residence immediately after they heard the bomb. The first time we inquired, he was gone and so was his personal stuff. It's like he never existed."

"Prints?"

"Sure, dozens. None identified as Levy's yet. We need a comparison."

"And you're pursuing other possible leads, right?"

"Sure. But you know how that goes."

"So how was the bomb triggered?"

"That's not certain yet. The BCA is doing more tests. But it looks like some kind of short-range radio signal triggered the device."

"Not the odometer as you first said?"

"There is still that odometer as a suspect. So we have several things to check out."

"Was that like a redundant system? Never heard of that, have you?" I stood up and dragged the phone toward the window that looks out on the side street.

"Not in these kinds of cases. 'Course, Roseville doesn't get a lot of bombings, you know?"

"Seems to me there's a possibility our prime candidate might be a patsy here." I looked at the baking roofs across the street one floor down, then farther down at the cars parked bumper to bumper along the street.

The Case of the Deceiving Don

"What are you saying?" Helen Lasker's voice became harsh in my ear. Cops universally don't like outsiders shaking the branches of their theoretical trees. "Are you holding out on me?"

"C'mon Sergeant. I would never do that and you know it. But if, just for a while, we assume that Levy didn't plant the bomb," I said, "it raises some interesting questions."

"Yeah? Like what?"

I saw a flicker of movement on the roof across the street. Maybe a janitor or somebody working out there. I turned away from the window and there was a ping, a tinkle and a thud. Now I didn't really hear all that as distinct separate sounds, they came too close together. But I know what a near miss feels like. I've been shot at before. I don't know exactly what I said when I shouted at Helen.

I dropped to my knees, dropped the phone and scuttled closer to the wall beside the window. When I raised my head just high enough to be able to see across the street again with one eye, the roof was empty. I looked up at my white ceiling. There was a dark spot on the plaster that hadn't been there before. A casual glance might lead one to believe it was a fly, a large horsefly, say. It wasn't. Perspiration leaked into my eyes. The phone squawked. I raised it to my ear in my sweaty hand.

"What?"

"Jesus, Sean, what just happened?"

"Somebody just shot at me!"

"Are you all right? Are you hit? What happened?"

"I'm okay. Somebody took a shot at me from the roof across the street."

"Shot?"

"Yeah, you know. Like, from a gun?"

"Are you hit?"

"No. Too short, I guess."

Chapter 10

The hole in my ceiling was a little larger now, and my bodily vibrations had lessened somewhat as the adrenalin rush subsided. But I was still wired. Several of Minneapolis's finest had come and gone. They dug the slug out of the ceiling, took a lot of pictures and told me I could patch the holes in the window and the plaster. I'd answered many questions, a lot of them repetitive, and spilled everything I knew about what I was working on at the moment. Since things were a little slow right then, that part of the conversation was brief. My only project at the moment was Molinaro. The detectives stated their opinions that the shooting was probably connected to the death of Molinaro. That big revelation didn't do much for my state of mind.

I'd called Catherine, and she was coming to the house in an hour or so. She'd wanted to rush over to my office immediately but I nixed that right off. If I was still being watched, I didn't want her linked to me. I realized they might have been following me and seen us at The Living Room the other night, but unless they'd done their homework, Catherine could have been tagged as just a casual date. We didn't need to make our relationship any more obvious than it was.

If I'd been a little more alert, I might have called in an ambulance and tried to fake my death or at least a grievous wound, but it was too late for that. The cops had verified that someone had been on the roof across the street and where the shooter had stood. Angles of entry and all that. Laser transits and so forth. Very cool technology. Didn't help my nerves at all.

While the cops were still in my office and checking the neighborhood, I measured my two windows, and after they all left, I called a place I found in the Yellow Pages that was close by and ordered some new window shades. I had blinds but they were old decrepit Venetian blinds that usually didn't work right. I was getting rid of the crappy blinds and putting in something else. I thought about nailing up some plywood sheets to cover the windows permanently, but that was impractical and the landlord would probably object. He sure as hell would at having to replace the glass. And anyway, I like having sunlight coming through the glass. When the sun shines.

I wasn't going to spend a lot of time on a separate investigation into finding the shooter. I figured I'd help the cops every possible way, but they have technical and other facilities far beyond mine for such things. Besides, I figured when I nailed the Don's bomber, the shooting would probably be cleared up at the same time. And if they got lucky and grabbed the shooter, well, it could only help me in my search for the bomber.

I sat at my desk and rubbed my fingers over the smooth wood edges. I stared at the wall and sort of thought about my life. Maybe I'd write some stuff down. Do a journal. This is what sometime happens when I have an unexpected jolt. I think about stuff and writing it down. I could write a novel. Something I haven't gotten around to.

It's different when I get into a confrontation with thugs. Where there's a threatening situation. Then there's a kind of build-up, so I'm prepared when the first bullet flies. Here there was no warning. I'm standing in the sunny window, calm as you please, talking on the phone when Bam! Bullet through the window. Unsettling, at the very least. So I rubbed the edge of my desk and thought about things. About my life.

That I would solve this bombing thing I had little doubt. I'm pretty good at what I do. Yeah, ego, I know, but I have a good track record. And because I am who I am and do what I do, you won't find a lot of information about me in the newspapers. Good private detectives are mostly anonymous. People hire me to get the goods, to find the facts. Truth and justice. Sometimes. That's what I do, and I mostly blend into the woodwork in the process. I'll go down those mean streets so you don't have to scuff up your shoes, mess up the creases in your pants.

Mostly, you won't know I've been there until long after I'm gone, if at all. I don't advertise. Not in the Yellow Pages. People who need me find me. I'm also short. Makes it difficult to follow people on a crowded street sometimes. On the other hand, my stature often leads my targets to underestimate me.

I don't go looking for trouble; that's too messy. But I do have a bag of tricks. I didn't qualify for the uniformed police force—too short. But that doesn't mean I don't know how to handle myself in a tight situation. I'm good with a handgun. With either hand. On the third hand, I rarely carry a firearm. I'm pretty well qualified in certain esoteric Eastern forms of passive-aggressive personal violence. I took the police academy course in baton twirling. I own a baton that I carry in the trunk of my car. Some mischievous fellows had occasionally found themselves in highly painful circumstances when they figured they were an easy match for me and my baton.

But the best thing I have going for me is flight. Marlowe probably wouldn't approve, but I figured out early on that I don't always need to bruise my knuckles on some thug's cheekbone, or sprain a thumb trying to disarm some brainless shooter. Zip. I'm outa there. There's another day a'coming. I can say, with a certain lack of modesty that most of the people I've come up against in six years of investigatory work are in the slammer if they should be.

Anyway. My hands stopped shaking, and I was now relatively

calm. I stopped rubbing the edge of my desk. I picked up the telephone again and called my buddy, a prosecutor in Ramsey County named Jerome Ford. We went back a long way, back to when he was a beat cop. We'd become close friends while he recovered from a .22 slug in the knee, a tumbling ricochet from a small time thief who was trying to rob an East Side liquor store.

"Jerry, I'm trying to run down some info on a minor league Mafia Don from the east coast."

"Molinaro? The guy who was blown up in Roseville?"

"That's the one."

"I figured the incident must have been close by from the address."

"Right across the street."

"What do you need, Sean?"

"Anything in your files? Haven't you got a few sources in OC taskforces who can give me some background? I can't recall anything that might be connected in the last fifteen years since the guy moved into the Sheltering Limbs retirement place."

"I might have a source. Isn't there a prime suspect?"

"Yes. His name is Martin Levy, and he's missing since the big boom."

"Okay, I'll see what I can dig up. But don't hold your breath."

We broke the connection, and I stood up and walked a tight circle around my desk. By now the slight tremors in my legs had also ceased so I could maneuver okay, but I didn't go near the window.

There came a knock, knock knocking on the door. I didn't exactly dive under the desk, but I suddenly felt real tense. "Yeah?"

"Mr. Sean, you called about some window blinds?"

"Okay, yeah. Wait a minute."

I took my piece out of the desk drawer and went to the door.

I cracked it open and peered out. The man standing there looked like what I expected, so I slid the gat into my pants pocket and let him in.

It was the blind guy from the window place. He came in, took some measurements and stuck his little finger on the bullet hole in the glass, but he didn't mention it. He told me that since I had standard windows, he had shades in stock.

"In fact, I got some in the truck that should fit. I'll just go get 'em."

"Sure," I said.

This time when he emerged from the elevator, carrying some blinds and his tool kit, I was standing outside my office in the hall, leaning against the wall. A careful observer might have noticed that I was right next to the door that led to the stairwell.

CHAPTER 11

Early the next morning, just as the sun was gilding the treetops along the eastern shore of Lake Johanna with a golden glow, I was swimming. I did several laps along the outer edge of the floats that identified the protected area off the north beach. I'd had a dreamless night, and the exercise felt good. Catherine was an advocate of swimming. She used the private pool in her building several times a week. Sometimes I went with her. I liked unchlorinated, natural water better, and I didn't mind that there were lots of tiny organisms floating right along with me. So that morning I swam back and forth just at the edge of the five-foot depth, until my arms and legs began to feel rubbery. Then I trudged out of the water and picked up my beach towel. I was alone on the beach, except for a woman several yards down the way. Wearing a two-piece swim suit, she was just sort of idling along, like a lot of people do on the beach, kicking at the sand. I couldn't tell what she looked like from that distance, but she seemed to have a pretty fair figure. Her short dark hair lifted slightly in the breeze from across the lake. I glanced down at my watch.

I had just time to get home, shower, eat and zip off to my surveillance assignment for the insurance company. This was a referral from a big hotshot law firm I'd been doing business with for years. In spite of the fact that I'd feuded with the late senior partner, Ephraim Harcourt Saint Martin, on a couple of occasions and nailed his firm for malfeasance, Harcourt, Saint

Martin, Saint Martin, Bryce et cetera continued to use my services for various jobs. I guess they liked my work. Anyway, right before the bombing of the Don, I had a call from an insurance investigator to check out an ex-employee who was creating problems.

Later that morning, after I saw my target, one Terry McGuire, off at the airport with his wife, I was back in my office. I hadn't actually seen the McGuire couple onto the plane, airport security being what it is, but I did verify their planned vacation with a couple of judicious calls. Their answering machine said they were away for a while and a neighbor confirmed for me that they were out of town for at least a week. Driving back from the airport, I glimpsed a couple of late-model Audis that were the right color. Or the wrong color, depending on your point of view. One silver-blue was going the opposite direction from me. The other followed me from the airport entrance east onto Highway 5 and then onto Fort Road leading into Saint Paul. But then it turned off at the first light.

I stopped downtown for a fried ham sandwich at Mickey's Diner, mixing in with several legal eagles and a government worker or two who frequented the place. After lunch I drove down University Avenue toward Minneapolis and my office. Traffic was normal for that time of day and nothing untoward happened, except I came within a hair of smacking a bus because I was studying a car in my rearview mirror. The target vehicle was the right color but I couldn't quite identify the make. When I looked up at the last second, the dirty white rear end of the bus was filling my windshield. I tromped on the brakes and executed a four-wheel smoking skid, stopping just in time. In fact I suspect that if the bus hadn't started forward at that moment I would have hit it. The vehicle I'd been staring at in my rearview mirror slid by on the right. It was silver-blue, but it wasn't an Audi.

I reversed the Taurus into my usual parking spot against the brick wall of the building where I had my office. I'd had to argue with the landlord for a few days to get the place. My parking spot had some advantages. It was only a few steps from the lobby door, so I could be behind the wheel and onto the street in moments. That was useful if I needed to trail someone from my office or get somewhere fast. A couple of years ago some miscreant tried to do me in with a bomb in my trunk. This arrangement left my trunk protected although the engine was more vulnerable. You make your choices, I guess.

Constantly alert to the passing parade, I glanced at cars parked along Central, in the lot, passing me. No silver-blue Audi. As I trotted into the building, I stumbled and almost decked a blond woman standing outside peering into the dim lobby.

"Excuse me," I said, clutching her padded shoulder. "I was looking the other way."

She shrugged and turned away.

Upstairs, my office was serene and untrammeled. I like that word. Untrammeled. I booted up my computer and went through the mail. A few bills, a bunch of ads and a check from a satisfied client. I wrote out deposit slips, signed checks, since my bank account was adequately funded at the moment and then I made a few notes. That mostly consisted of contact queries and dates. I wasn't getting very far very fast figuring out who had offed the Don and why.

I took a look at one of my detective training manuals. What would Lew Archer do in my situation? I pulled a Ross Mac-Donald pocket book from my bottom drawer. I skimmed several chapters which served to remind me what a good writer Mac-Donald was, but it didn't help my present situation a whole lot. Archer did suggest that in his experience, at least, old crimes seemed to be at the root of much of his clients' troubles. When the telephone rang, I picked up. That turned out to be one of my poorer decisions of the day.

It was the Roseville PD on the line. Sergeant Helen Lasker to be precise.

"Mr. Sean," she said.

Right away, see, I knew something big was going down.

"Yes ma'am," I responded. "How may I be of service?"

"Some questions have come up. Is it possible for you to come out here? We—I'd like to talk to you as soon as possible."

Her formality and tone of voice told me two things. First there was somebody with her, close enough to hear at least her side of the conversation. And secondly, whatever she wanted, it was heavy. She was giving me a chance to become abruptly unavailable, to hide, if you will, should I so desire.

"Can you tell me why?" I ventured.

"I'd prefer we discuss this face to face, if you don't mind. And it is rather urgent."

Aha, I thought. "I haven't anything pressing the rest of the afternoon. I can be there in an hour. How's that?"

"Acceptable, but earlier if you can. Thank you, Mr. Sean."

So I cleared off my desk, logged a few things into the computer and shut it down. At my car I glanced warily around. No silver-blue Audi. No one who might be giving me the eye. No one aiming a weapon in my direction. No one at all. I took off for Roseville, timing my arrival at the cop shop in our Lexington Avenue City Hall for a little less than thirty minutes later.

When I got to the reception window and stated my business, a detective I didn't know came around the barrier to open the security lock. He ushered me back to the small conference room, instead of Helen Lasker's cubicle. He rapped once on the door and then stood aside to let me walk in.

Sergeant Lasker was seated at the end of the table farthest

from the door. Standing against the wall on the other side of the room were two men, neatly groomed in upscale dark suits and brilliant white shirts. They were both armed, wearing shoulder holsters under carefully sculpted coats. Feds, I thought to myself.

Chapter 12

I nodded at Sergeant Lasker and raised one eyebrow as I swung my gaze to the two strangers. "Federales," I said. "Very interesting." I was not imitating Arte Johnson.

Helen nodded in their direction. "Agent Dutton and Agent Arista. From our local FBI office."

"You could have saved yourselves a trip out here to our 'burb, you know. I have an office near downtown Minneapolis, after all." I slid into a chair across the table. Agent Dutton pulled out another chair and sat. Agent Arista remained standing. Both men seemed relaxed but watchful. There was a moment of silence.

I looked at Helen Lasker. "So? What's the deal?"

She shrugged and said, "Ask them. I'm just cooperating with our federal colleagues here."

Agent Dutton cleared his throat and said quietly, "We understand you're a private investigator."

I nodded.

"And you live at this address where a certain Augustus Molinaro died a few days ago. Correct?"

"Almost. I wasn't home when it happened, but the evidence suggests that the explosion that killed Mr. Molinaro occurred directly across the street from my place."

"Yes."

"So technically, I guess you'd have to say it happened at a different address but in close proximity to my address."

"And what was the damage to your house?"

"None that I can see. I mean, no new cracks in the plaster. No windows broken, nothing uprooted or burned in the yard. I think Mr. Hopkins had a broken window, though. He lives at the address in front of which the death occurred. Hopkins is my neighbor."

"And you were not acquainted with the victim, is that correct?"

"Yes, that's correct."

"And you weren't aware he was residing in the Sheltering Limbs at the time of his death?"

"That's also correct."

"What about Martin Levy? Did you know him?"

"No."

"Have you any information as to Mr. Levy's present whereabouts?" the agent asked.

" 'Fraid not."

"Do you have an idea who would have wanted to kill Mr. Molinaro?"

"No."

"Have you provided the police with the names and descriptions of any possible witnesses you observed while you were at the scene?"

"Yes." I was getting a mite impatient. I knew Sergeant Lasker had already provided the information they were asking about, and they could tell they weren't going to trip me into some variation. Why were we wasting time?

"Mr. . . . Sean." The agent paused. That happens sometimes. Because my name is Sean Sean, people aren't always sure just how to address me. Calling me by my first name at this stage of the interrogation was probably not in the FBI quiz manual. So there was that little pause. The agent wasn't sure whether he was using my first or my last name.

"Look, Agent . . . Dutton." I hesitated just a bit to let him know I'd noticed his pause, then said, "Why don't you come right out and say what's on your mind. As I'm sure Sergeant Lasker has already informed you, I tend to take a cooperative attitude toward law enforcement types, long as they don't try to lean on me unreasonably."

Both agents stared at me. I bet they were thinking that, given my diminutive size, they could throw their weight advantage around pretty well. Agent Dutton nodded.

"Point taken, Mr. Sean. What we are wondering is that since you seem to have only peripheral interest in this death, why do we keep encountering your name or your presence as investigations of the case move forward."

Interest is right. They apparently didn't know I had a client. Including Helen Lasker, I'd been talking to several police agencies in the metro area. Now I had to figure they'd all ratted me out to these federal boys. I was going to be more circumspect in the future. I also wondered at his use of investigations, plural.

"Well, you might say that since the guy died practically on my doorstep, I'm taking a neighborly interest in helping Roseville's finest clean up the mess. What I mean is, who knows how many other nefarious characters like Greasy Gus are being quietly housed in our community? Isn't this something that civic-minded citizens ought to take to City Hall? I mean, do I have to start worrying about property values?"

Lasker hid a grin while the agents looked dead serious. "I believe, Mr. Sean, we can assure you there are no other, as you put it, nefarious characters residing in Roseville's assisted living centers, at least, none of whom we're aware." Agent Dutton rose and said to Sergeant Lasker, "Thanks for your help, Sergeant. Good luck with your investigation. Thanks for coming in, Mr. . . . Sean."

It was clear to me that FBI Agent Dutton and his silent

shadow didn't think the Roseville PD was going to open any worm cans in their attempts to solve Gus Molinaro's murder. It also appeared they weren't the people in the silver-blue Audi who were shadowing me. Unless they were really good actors. Maybe it was another federal agency. Even though post 9/11 there was supposed to be a whole lot more interagency co-operation, scuttlebutt on the street said it wasn't happening.

I waited there in the conference room until Lasker returned from seeing her federal visitors to the lobby security door. When she reappeared she said, "Well?"

"Interesting. Why were they here?"

"Courtesy, mostly. Far as we know, there's no federal crime here."

I nodded. "Far as we know. Do you get the feeling they've dismissed us? Was there anything of importance in your chat with the boys before I got here?"

Lasker shook her head. "No. We covered a few details of the investigation you already know about, and they gave me some new contacts in the FBI to call if I thought they could help with this and future events."

"Do you think they knew Gus was living in Roseville?"

"Hard to say, Sean, but my guess is no."

I remained seated.

"Something else?" she said.

"About that pot shot at me yesterday." Just mentioning it out loud, and I could feel my body heating up. It had been a close shave.

"Do you figure whoever tried for the hit is connected to the Molinaro bombing?"

"Yeah, I do. Sure, there are a couple of creeps out there who'd like to punch my lights out, but nobody, even from years past, who could bring that kind of heat is in any position to do it."

She frowned. "You sure?"

"Pretty sure. Almost a hundred percent. And I'm being shadowed."

"The Audi?"

"Yeah. I've seen it more than a couple of times. There's nothing else going on in my life right now that even approaches that level of malfeasance, so it must be this Molinaro thing. I'm reminding you because you're leading the local investigation, which means you're more exposed than usual."

"Maybe so. Did you see that bit on the news about the guy who shot his own attorney because he didn't like the way the case was decided? That was some sort of tax thing."

"Yeah. But that was California. Watch yourself, Ms. Lasker."

We stared at each other in silence for another long moment. "Thanks for the reminder," she said softly.

I got out of there. No silver-blue Audi awaited me in the parking lot, and I didn't see anyone pointing a rifle my way.

Chapter 13

At home, my answering device was active. The message-received light blinked steadily. I don't have a cell phone, although I'm thinking about getting one. I figure telephones are for my convenience, not the caller's. Yeah, I know, I can turn it on or off, but suppose I forget to turn it off and I'm sneaking around quiet-like, or I get into a tense stand-off situation and the damn thing rings, or beeps or whatever it's set to? It would be distracting and even embarrassing, not to say possibly fatal. So I don't have one. Yet.

The lone message, from my detective friend R. Simon at the Minneapolis PD, told me that Martin Levy, aka Martino Johnson, aka Martin Levine, was mobbed up in a remote kind of way. He was also a dangerous fella and assumed to be armed. A BOLO had been issued, Ricardo told my audio tape. I knew that means be on the lookout. Levy has, apparently, no known local friends or fellow felon acquaintances. That's gonna make him harder to find. I am, however, persistent. I decided to call in some favors.

I freshened the cats' water, locked up, and went to my office. There I called Sal Bellasario. He's a local real estate mover and property owner. That's what he does on the surface. Below the surface he scuffles about in all kinds of somewhat shady deals. He's also a go-between. He goes between pretty much anyone who can meet his price and somebody else. I occasionally do things for him, but we aren't best buds. A voice says he's in at

Triple A Realty.

"Sal. How they hanging?"

"Sean, will you quit with the slangy stuff? It doesn't fit your image. What can I do for you this time?" I heard him hack and then wheeze. He still smoked evil black cigarillos. That's part of his image, even though I happened to know his doctor has told him to lay off the things.

"I'm looking for a guy."

"So tell me something new. I'm busy here, you know? I have things to do and places to go."

"Sal, Sal, listen. The gent I'm looking for uses the name Martin Levy. He worked in town for several years as a personal attendant to a guy living in a retirement home."

"Who was the old man?"

"Augustus Molinaro."

"Greasy Gus?" Sal interrupted. "Sure. He's sometimes known as Don Molinaro, although he wasn't particularly large in the OC scene."

"You know him?"

"Of him, my friend. Of him. I don't associate myself with the families if I can avoid it. I prefer to stay as far as possible from that whole scene. Live and let live, I say." He stopped babbling long enough to hack three times into my ear. Then I heard him noisily inhaling one of his black coffin nails.

"Those things are gonna kill you, Sal."

"This or somethin' else."

"So can you help?"

"Let me make a few calls." He hung up the phone before I could say anything else.

I went to the window and put my little finger in the hole in the glass pane where the rifle bullet had struck. It wasn't that I hadn't been shot at before, although it wasn't a frequent thing. But those times were always in the heat of the chase. I was sometimes shooting back. This shooting incident, as one cop had called it, was a case of cold, plotted, assassination. That's a whole other thing, and I don't mind admitting it shook me a little. So I stuck my finger in the hole to sort of remind myself to be careful. I didn't stand in front of the window while I did it, either.

I knew I had to get the Audi off my back. It was hampering my activities and giving me a persistent crick in the neck. I went down the hall to my neighbor ladies, the cousins Revulon. Betsey and Belinda, tall, shapely Scandinavian ladies, had far more expertise in computer-land than I, and I thought they could help me out.

"Good afternoon," I said opening the door to their summons after rapping on the glass. Belinda, slouched in her black, ergonomically designed, leather covered executive chair, had her feet up on the table. Her slim ankles were crossed and the short skirt she was wearing provided any visitor with a fine view of her long, elegantly shaped, smooth legs. She cradled a wireless keyboard in her lap. The sound in her earphones was loud enough I figured she was going deafer by the minute. She grinned up at me, fingers flying over the keys. After a couple of minutes she stopped typing, killed the CD sound, and set the keyboard on the table beside her. She left her ankles where they were.

"Hey, Sean Sean, my fav detective. Is this a social or a business visit?"

Both women had, somewhere right after they moved into this office, decided I needed mothering, even though they were both younger than I. It wasn't a romantic thing—they knew about and liked Catherine and wouldn't dream of trying to poach on her territory.

"Business, strictly business. What I need is to learn about a certain automobile. A car."

"Sure. Got any details?"

"The target is a late model, probably this year or last. It's a silver-blue four-door Audi sedan with tinted windows. I don't have the license plate yet, but it's definitely Minnesota."

"Okay, and you want to know what?"

"First, how many are registered and if it's not a huge number, ownership details. Can do?"

"Sure, hon. I'll get one of our search bots on it right away. Anything else?"

There wasn't, so I left. Regretfully, because the scenery in my office was a lot less interesting.

I called Rick Simon, my cop friend. He wasn't in, naturally, so I left a message on his voice mail reminding him about the bombing death of Don Molinaro and my search for his erstwhile companion. Then I booted up my desktop computer and read my emails. That much I can do with assurance.

I can also type in notes on my cases and print out client bills. But that's about it when it comes to computerland. Most of the forty messages were spam. I hate that label. I actually enjoy an occasional sandwich of Hormel's Spam. The crap messages got deleted. None of the remaining emails required any action on my part, except filing or erasing which I also could do and did. Then I went to my notes on the case and added my interview with the FBI guys and the questions it raised in my mind, like why were they interested and how many investigations were going on and to whom did the damn Audi belong? That document I saved again on a floppy. I don't know why they're called floppies, being hard plastic shells. I don't leave anything I consider private in my office machine. I have a stack of floppies that I stash in secret places. It's inconvenient, but when the Revulon cousins were persuading me to buy a computer, and the question of protection came up, they explained passwords and encryption and lost me after the second sentence. It was too much gobbledygook so I adopted a more practical approach of never leaving sensitive stuff in my computer. It's also obvious when you boot it up that there are no encrypted files. It's the electronic equivalent of stores that leave their registers open so burglars won't damage expensive machines breaking into empty cash drawers. Yes, I have since learned that even files long erased can be recovered if one has the right programs and sufficient expertise. But there are limits. The chances of my having files that were of such sensitivity were miniscule, and I wasn't going to bankrupt myself with elaborate security to protect against a 500-year flood.

Chapter 14

It was time to leave. I took a cautious peek out my window at the street below. Nothing suspicious. I scanned the roof across the street and the few windows that looked into what appeared to be empty rooms. I stepped into the hall, quickly glancing in both directions. I saw that the Revulon cousins' office was dark. They must have already left for the day. Looking more relaxed than I felt, I elevatored to the main lobby, but instead of exiting onto the street, I took a more circuitous route through the building to a back door that opened into the refuse and pickup ramp where the trash and recycle containers were stored.

I avoided kicking any cans and picked my way cautiously around the building to my parking space. I saw nothing suspicious enroute. No silver-blue Audi, no rifle muzzle, no one and no thing. My Taurus was tight against the brick wall. I risked damage to my slacks and got down to look under the car. Then I reached under the radiator grille and popped the hood. It's a little modification I've had done. No evidence of tampering. Even better, no bundle of dynamite wired to the starter. So I hopped in and took off for the Kenwood district of Minneapolis where I knew my lady love was waiting.

Catherine lived in a pretty secure building, and she'd been able to lease a second underground parking stall. We'd originally planned for a night out, but given the bullet hole in my window, I wasn't about to chance exposing Catherine to some fool with an itchy trigger finger and an inflated belief in his accuracy.

The Case of the Deceiving Don

Traffic on the freeways was getting thick so I opted for city streets. More stop and go with the lights, but it seemed as if I was getting somewhere faster. More illusion, I suspected, but I preferred it to crawling in traffic on a sun-blasted strip of concrete with fumes from a thousand engines rising around me.

On the other hand, sitting in slow-moving traffic occasionally gave me time to think. Usually about whatever case I was on, but sometimes about other things. One of my recurring themes of late was My Life. Whither was I going? I knew a couple of long-time P.I.s. Once in a great while we'd get together and hoist a few. One was Duke Fararra, my original mentor, the guy I'd interned under. That's necessary in Minnesota in order to qualify for an operator's license. We often talked about where we were going. Duke Fararra had no such questions by the time I got to know him. He was entrenched and comfortable in his niche.

It had been a while since I'd last talked to Duke. Maybe six months, maybe a year. The last time I'd been in South Saint Paul, once home of the largest stockyards between Chicago and the West Coast, on an insurance job. On a whim I stopped in to see him. He was there all right. Sitting in his high-backed leather chair, he peered near-sighted at me when his nubile receptionist/secretary ushered me in to the great man's sanctum. He didn't get up. He never rose to greet visitors of any stripe. I reached across his massive antique rosewood desk to shake his limp hand.

"So, Mr. Sean. I am delighted to see you this afternoon, my boy."

"I was in the neighborhood, Duke, so I thought I'd take a chance you were in."

"In the neighborhood?" His thin eyebrows rose a fraction. "Really?"

"Nothing substantial." I waved my hand dismissively. Poaching on what Fararra considered his home territory was not done. "Just a routine insurance query."

Fararra brushed non-existent lint from his silk smoking jacket.

I pushed my dark fedora to the back of my head and said, "I haven't a whole lot of time, you know. Busy for some reason."

"Ah, well, the miscreants are thick upon the ground these days, or so it would appear. You're still in the business then? Have you no plans to retire or move on to something more worthwhile, shall we say? Something more stimulating and more significant perhaps?"

Duke was always on me to get out of the business. It was either his attempt to push me into something that would give full rein to what he called my 'undeniable talents,' or he just wanted to get rid of some of the competition.

Through the wall of his office I could hear that the telephone seemed to be constantly ringing. "I guess you're pretty busy yourself. I was going to suggest we go next door for a drink." His office was next door to a dark quiet bar on El Gatos Street and only two blocks from the old Cattlemen's Hotel with its big nineteenth-century decor watering hole.

"Thanks, dear boy, I'm just not available right now, but surely we can have a rain check?"

Thinking about it now, I realized that drop-in was over a year ago and I hadn't talked to him since. I should call. Of course the rascal could call me. He knew how to use the telephone, even if he no longer had one in his office. I wheeled left out of the sun and hit the button on the garage door opener that let me into the cavernous parking garage beneath Catherine's posh apartment building. The elevator was waiting, and I whisked up four flights, down the long carpeted hall and, with my own key, entered her pad.

It was a very comfortable apartment with three nice-sized bedrooms, one of which she used as an office. The smallest was her exercise room fitted out with, among other things, the nicest massage table I had ever seen. Not that I'm expert on such accoutrements. She is.

"I'm in the playroom, honey." Her voice floated down the hall to where I was getting a glass of cold water from the refrigerator.

"Want a drink?"

"Nope. Not now. We'll have wine with dinner, I think."

I strolled toward her with a glass in my hand, stopping in the small bedroom to put my gat and shoulder holster in the cabinet there. Ever since somebody tried to pot me in my office I'd taken to going about heeled. Here we were on the fourth floor of a building with rent-a-cops on duty 24/7. I felt secure. Pretty secure. And I knew Catherine didn't like guns. Although I also knew she had one stashed in her built-in safe in the bedroom, or playroom as she had nick-named it since I'd arrived on the scene.

She was standing before the full-length mirror next to her closet wearing only filmy underthings and black high heels. The gown she was holding up was a floor length sheath in some kind of aqua material that caught highlights in her eyes. I could see that even from all the way across the room where I was standing at the door.

She cut her eyes at me and smiled. "New dress I just picked up at Elissa's downtown. You like?"

"Put it on."

Catherine shook her head. "Later, babe. I tried it on at the shop. Now I just wanted to see it in this light."

"You're a knockout, in or out of that dress."

She turned away and switched her firm fanny at me while she replaced the dress in her closet. "You say the nicest things." Then she threw on a big lightweight white tee and a pair of maroon shorts, shedding the heels at the same time. Barefoot she padded to me and placed her arms around my neck. I reciprocated, and we smooched in the doorway for a few minutes.

"Dinner," she breathed, "is almost ready. We need a nice red wine. Would you be so kind?"

I was and I did. A few minutes later I discovered she'd put together one of her famous—to me anyway—French cookbook stews. I have no idea what all was in the stew except savory gravy, tender beef, and some interesting vegetables all dolled up with herbs and spices. On the side we enjoyed a crisp salad of romaine, cheese, tender tomatoes, and a very light dressing.

"Terrific, my dear," I mumbled around another mouthful from my second bowl. "What do you call this dish?"

"*Casserole ala Mckerney,* what else?"

Wine in hand we adjourned to the living room where we entwined limbs and watched the late news.

Chapter 15

"What's up on your social calendar in the next month or so?" I asked. The news was a fading memory, and we were getting ready for bed.

"I have nothing out of the routine for a couple of weeks at least. We do have that library board fund raiser though. That's why I bought the dress."

"When is that?"

"Last Saturday of the month. The twenty-third, I think."

I nodded, slipping between the cool sheets. "Okay. I should be clear by then."

Catherine joined me, nude, our usual sleeping garb. Her cool hand snaked out and fondled my chest. "You did agree, you know."

"Oh, I'm up for it. I just don't like the idea of going into a big public gathering while I still have a target pinned to my ass."

"The Molinaro thing?"

"The Molinaro thing. Ordinarily my work doesn't interfere with your social stuff, you know that."

"Well, I know if I didn't push you a little, you wouldn't have much of a social life at all."

I could hear the smile in her voice. She rose on one elbow and leaned close, giving me a dimly lit glimpse of her bare breasts under the tented sheet. I started to roll toward her and felt her wrist lock as she pushed her palm against my chest.

"Sttst, lover," she murmured. "Sleep now." Her soft lips brushed mine and we both lay back down.

The next morning I was up at six. The sun was garnishing the tall tree-tops and the buildings to the east. Catherine was still sleeping, snuffling softly, the sheet tangled around her thighs. I kissed her bare hip, grabbed a big towel and slipped into the bathroom to don my swimming trunks, a robe, and slide into rubber flip-flops. In the basement I found the pool empty of other humans. I dove in and began a slow series of laps. Twenty minutes later I dragged myself out of the end of the pool. Only then did I discover I'd forgotten my key to the apartment. Rats. Well, no matter, the house phone on the wall of the pool room connected me to Catherine, five floors above. The phone rang and rang and then the answering machine kicked in.

Shoot. I went into the shower and soaped off the chemically-saturated pool water and went back to the phone. Again, it rang and rang and there was no answer. Hell. She couldn't have already left the apartment. She wouldn't do that without saying goodbye. Would she? A small *frisson* of alarm ticked into my mind. I went to the elevator and up to the garage. Her car was still in its stall. I reentered the elevator and punched the button for the main floor. The guard at the desk frowned at my lack of street clothes and told me he hadn't seen Ms. Mckerney and no one had gone in for the last hour or so. I was only slightly relieved.

Back in the elevator I rose to the fourth floor. The fourth floor was deathly quiet. I shed my flip-flops and trotted silently down the hall, robe flapping around my calves. With infinite care I turned the knob. Damn. The door was unlocked. Easing it slowly open I smelled coffee and something else I couldn't identify. There were no sounds from the apartment. I padded quietly across the empty living room and past the dining table to the kitchen door. The coffee smell was stronger. My stomach was in a knot.

I stuck my head slowly around the kitchen door jamb.

Catherine turned her head and smiled. "Hey, have a good swi—what's wrong? Has something happened?"

My breath, which I'd been unconsciously holding for some seconds, whooshed out of me. "I was afraid"—I gestured, unable to continue for a moment. "God, when you didn't answer the phone either time—I thought—I don't know *what* I thought." I shook my head, relief washing through me.

Catherine slid off her stool and came to me, throwing her arms around my neck. "Oh, baby, I'm so sorry. I must have been in the shower when you called." She squeezed my neck and kissed my cheek. "When I got out of bed I saw your key on the dresser, so I unlatched the front door. I never heard the phone at all."

I hugged her close and kissed her neck, relief so strong it left me trembling. We stood locked together for some moments. Eventually I pulled back just a little and craned a look up at her face. "I guess that rifle shot across my bow has still got me freaked. But I'll take this, any time."

Catherine smiled down into my eyes and whacked me lightly on the shoulder. "You be careful out there, you hear?" Then she stepped out of my arms. "There's juice, coffee, and a bagel on the counter. Spreads are in the refrigerator in the usual spot. Can you find them? We overslept and now I have to run."

I let her go, and she brushed my cheek again with her lovely lips. Then she grabbed her purse and zipped out the door. After she closed the door I realized she'd never said those words to me before. A measure of her concern, I guess.

She knew I'd been shot at in earlier years. She saved my life once, from a slightly berserk attorney, and it wasn't too long ago she'd been the target of some thugs who'd thought they could get rid of me by attacking Catherine. It hadn't worked. But I know life is fragile, even for the ordinary person who doesn't deal with thieves and other assorted low-lifes on a regular basis.

I leaned closer to the plate of bagels. There was the smell I'd detected. An onion bagel which I detest and avoid at all times. I threw it in the garbage.

I had no compelling reason to be at the office immediately so I settled at Catherine's desk and called Ricardo Simon at the MPD. He was in.

"Hey, my friend, what can you tell me about the progress of the MPD investigation into the shooter at my office?"

"Coincidentally," he responded, "I was wondering the same thing, so I have here the report. The projectile they took out of your ceiling was pretty badly distorted after going through two panes of glass and into a few inches of paint and plaster. The slug is so distorted it's useless in identifying the exact weapon from which it was fired. However, the lab believes the slug to be a .30-06 Winchester manufacture."

"A hunting rifle?"

"Could be. No brass was found where the shooter was standing. We did locate a couple of cigarette butts. If they belong to the shooter, we'll have DNA for comparison once somebody comes up with a suspect. We don't have a report back from the BCA's DNA database yet."

"I guess you aren't sure the butts and the shooter are connected."

"True enough, Sean. The roof is accessible, and the landlord admits teenagers and others sometimes hang out up there."

"Ok, thanks. It doesn't sound like a professional hitter, does it?"

"Not so far. Complicates things perhaps."

"Yeah, it may not be tied to Greasy Gus at all."

Chapter 16

After I hung up I thought about that rifle shot some more. On the one hand, professional hit persons—you couldn't just call them men anymore since a couple of women out East had turned out to be experienced shootists—settle into a groove. They're like the rest of us, they go with the known and the familiar. Their known and familiar just happens to be stalking and assassinating. Okay, so Doc Holliday liked smooth-bore shotguns because he didn't have to aim precisely. Somebody using a rifle was more likely to keep using the same weapon and the same ammo if only because the distances involved required a familiar weapon with known characteristics. Assassins didn't want to go to the trouble of getting comfortable with an expensive new weapon every time they took a contract if they didn't have to. Besides buying new rifles would cut into their bottom line. Unlike Doc Holliday, modern killers, when engaged in personal assassinations, frequently use cheap handguns which are easily replaced.

And word apparently gets around. That's why there was a rash of Mafia hits in which the killers each used a .22 caliber revolver for close-up work. Head shots. Low power weapons such as a .22 don't make much noise. The slug goes into the subject's head and rattles around, plowing furrows in various important parts of the brain. The slug is so distorted it's frequently useless for forensics and since a revolver doesn't eject the cartridge, there's no brass left at the scene. Cheap revolvers are more reliable than cheap semi-automatics. So what did that all mean? It might mean the shooter was not a pro contractor and was using a personal weapon. It might mean the shooter was known to me. It might not mean any of those things.

Thinking those uplifting thoughts, I went to the small closet in the second bedroom and pulled out a new pair of red tennis shoes. I'm partial to Keds, and when, a few years ago, they terminated the brand, I bought several dozen pairs. The ones with white soles and accents. I figure with normal wear and tear, I have enough pairs to last me a lifetime. So I donned white cotton socks and laced up a new pair of high tops. I was ready to face the world.

Another thought occurred. If the rifleperson who'd missed me was an expert, I either was damn lucky or the shooter might have been trying to miss—firing a shot across my bow, so to say. Or, it could be a really smart perp using non-standard killing equipment in order to mask the professional doing the shooting.

I slipped on my armpit basket-weave holster and took my revolver out of the cabinet. I was going about town armed. My gun, my gat, was a very nice Smith and Wesson model 331 revolver. It carried .32 caliber H&R Magnum rounds. My pistol was only a bit over six inches in length and weighed less than a pound. A small weapon for a small guy. Lethal though. Since I got shot at, I wasn't going anywhere without being heeled, and I could carry this little S&W all day and hardly notice it was there, unless I needed it. It didn't have the stopping power or the accuracy of my big Colt semi-auto, but up close and personal, it was every bit as deadly.

I elevatored to the basement, scanned the environs, and went to my car. No Audis of any color anywhere in sight. I checked under the car and the hood for any explosive devices. Finding none, I hopped aboard and drove through downtown, past the

The Case of the Deceiving Don

big placid skyscrapers and out Central to my modest five-floor office building.

There appeared to be nothing amiss outside, so I walked down the hall to my neighbors, the computer experts, the Revulon cousins. They were ready for me.

"Hey, good morning Mr. Sean," crowed Betsey, thrusting her prominent bosom at me as she twisted around the crowded space. Her hand came out and we slapped palms.

"And good morning to you," I responded. "Have you found out anything useful?"

"You bet. Today there is good news and not so good news."

"Lay it on me."

"Here," said Belinda, emerging from the back room, also crowded with electronic machines and gadgets, "is a report of the automobiles you asked about."

It was a thin stack of papers. The printing was single-spaced. One-and two-year-old Audi sedans registered in the state of Minnesota. Without looking at the count, it was painfully obvious there were hundreds. "What about the color?" I asked.

"That's the better news," said Belinda, producing another, smaller report. "There are about two dozen ice-blue Audis registered in the state. After we got the raw data, I segmented the search. Here are separate lists of the machines in question registered to rental agencies, leased autos and corporate and individual owners." She kept placing single and multiple-page reports in my outstretched hands.

"Very nice," I said, thinking this may not be a completely unmanageable task after all. None of the breakdowns were so large that I couldn't deal with them single-handed. I wouldn't have to call in any favors or hire any troops.

"You'll find some anomalies," Betsey commented.

"Some what?"

"Some of the entries on the comprehensive list don't appear

anywhere else."

"Some of the entries on the breakouts don't appear on the comprehensive list," added Belinda.

"Why is that?"

"Inevitable, Sean. Streams of data running through the ether often shed bits and pieces. And if the databases we hacked—er queried—were in use at the time, some entries might have been skipped or garbled. Howsomever, life is good and we think we got a 95% accuracy rate." She smiled her dazzling white smile at me.

"Thank you, ladies, I appreciate your efforts on behalf of truth and justice."

We smiled at each other and I took the load of paper to my office.

I decided that some of the entries could be quickly eliminated at least for the time being. I lined out corporate owners or lessees that I recognized. I strongly doubted that any of the security people at Carlson Companies, for example, would be gunning for me—or anybody else. Marilyn Nelson might be a tough boss in the board room, but she simply wasn't the kind of CEO to resort to murder. Besides, we had no connection. Zero.

No government agencies like the DEA or the FBI showed up on the list. Of course, the government has a penchant for creating new agencies or offices at the drop of a dime, and I wouldn't recognize some of them. Plus, if I was encountering a truly clandestine agency with operatives shadowing li'l ol' me, I wouldn't know it anyway. Things like that I only speculate on. I can't worry about something beyond my ken.

When I finished eliminating the remotest of the remote and the merely illogical and generally remote, I was left with twenty-five possibles, all with addresses in the five county region. Telephone and leg-work were up next.

Chapter 17

I called all twenty-five. One was a really grumpy guy.

"Yeah? Who is this?"

He was breathing heavily into the phone. I figured either I woke him up or he'd just run up from the basement.

"Good morning, Mr. Jones. This is Cotton Mather with Worldwide Marketing. We're calling Audi owners for purposes of determining their level of satisfaction with the automobile. Do you still own the late model ice-blue four-door Audi?"

"Yeah, so?"

"And do you drive it regularly?"

"Yeah, but not the last two days. Somebody slashed two tires, and I'm waiting for the insurance company to come get it."

"I see. Thanks very much for your time." I hung up on his continual mumble. My calls eliminated ten for sure and five more probables. I figured the five that were kid or female chatty sorts of answering machine messages were safe deletions. Another five were small companies that turned out to be in the Yellow Pages. If they were in the Yellow Pages they had to have been around a while, considering that it takes more than a year to get a listing into a published Yellow Pages book.

I swung my white and red Keds off the desk and locked up. List of culled addresses in hand, I sortied forth. As I stepped from the building's back door into the alley, I scanned alley, parking lot and nearby street. All seemed serene. I glanced under my car and then under the hood. I was getting tired of this routine.

I am a normally careful driver except when in hot pursuit, something that's happened twice in my years as a P.I. I was being even more careful, scanning intersections and keeping one eyeball glued to the rearview mirror for ice-blue Audis. It was an uncomfortable stance. Plus, my skin under the shoulder holster itched.

I'd laid out a route, allowing the least amount of road time to get from one to the other of my target owners. As I pulled up to the first address, a private home almost in Robbinsdale, a northwest suburb, I felt my stomach clench when I caught sight of the Audi parked at the curb. Well, of course. That's what I was looking for. The house was a small fifties-era cottage. It had a well-kept lot and exterior, but didn't seem like the kind of place one expected to find an expensive ride. The car was parked at the curb. It was the right model and the right year, but it was dusty and looked like it could use a good wash. I glanced in the back seat to discover a blanket of some kind wadded up in one corner and what appeared to be some kid litter on the floor. The side windows were dirty and it sure didn't look like an assassin's car. Disguise? I didn't think so.

A window air conditioner banged away on my left. The woman who opened the front door to my knock was in her late forties. She wore an apron with flour on it. Her hands were floury too and her smudged tennis shoes were untied. She had trim ankles. I flashed my honorary Ramsey County Sheriff's badge at her and asked a couple of neutral questions about kids loitering in the neighborhood recently. She didn't have any idea and no complaints. My visit didn't seem to worry her. I thanked her and left. Unusual, to find a woman at home doing domestic tasks.

And so it went for several of the other privately owned vehicles. Several obvious retirees. In a few places, there was no answer to my knock and no evidence of the Audis on the street or in the garages where I poked around. Not surprising. People do go to work. The neighborhoods ranged from modest to upscale homes. I penciled in question marks on my list.

Then I started on the firms. Twice I found ice-blue Audi sedans parked in reserved spots in the open ground-level parking lots of company buildings. In one I talked my way into the underground parking garage. Alas, no Audi. In Edina I went looking for a company with the enigmatic name, The Elite Corporation. The building was one of those modern glass affairs with tinted blue all-glass walls through which you couldn't see anything except at night when the lights were on. After reconnoitering the lot, I parked in the visitors section and sauntered into the lobby through one of four revolving door sets.

It being late afternoon, the sun behind the building gave the vast lobby a kind of unhealthy shadowless glow. This lobby was an eight-story atrium, ending at a ceiling with cloudy glass panels through which the blue sky, spotted with a few white puffs, was fuzzily visible. The floor was highly polished greenish marble. I squeaked as I walked toward the big bronze-colored relief on the opposite wall. In the center of the sculpture was a panel with brass nameplates of the firms ensconced in the building. There it was, Elite, and a number, 820, which I assumed meant they were on the eighth floor. The elevator column was almost directly ahead of me so I started in that direction. More squeaking from my new Keds.

"Excuse me, sir."

The heavy voice came from a burly man standing behind a curved, waist high wall of some sort. Ah, I thought, the information aka security desk. I'd noticed the desk, of course, but there hadn't been anyone there when I'd entered the lobby. Or he'd been hiding.

I turned toward the speaker. "Yes?" I said. "Can I help you?"

Startled by his usual question being pre-empted, the burly man, in what I now saw was a blue suit over a blue shirt and a plain blue tie, a uniform, perhaps, looked at me, saying nothing. In that moment I could have gone on by but I didn't.

"Yes, sir," I said. "I'm on my way to the Elite Company on eight. Is there a problem?"

"Appointment?" he said, hefting a padded three-ring binder up from the desk concealed behind his wall. By now I was only a step away from the wall. The guard, I assumed he was, wasn't wearing a weapon that I could detect. That either meant he had a really good tailor, which I doubted, or he wasn't armed, or the weapon was in the desk.

I make it a practice to be nice in these situations. Why not? This guy wasn't aggressive, he was just doing his job. So far. "No appointment. I don't even have a name, but I do have business with them."

The guard looked down at the sheet in front of him. He shook his head. "Nope, nobody gets up there without an appointment."

"Well, can we call someone right now?" I didn't see a phone, but I was sure he had one.

"Nope, no calls."

"Look," I pleaded. "I came all the way out here. Can't we just try?"

There was noise behind me and I looked around to see a tall well-dressed man with a woman in a trim business suit beside him stride into the lobby. They headed for the elevators. The red-head waved casually toward us. Out of the corner of my eye, I saw the guard acknowledge her. I turned back.

"So, what do you suggest?"

He shrugged and said nothing. I considered offering the man a bribe, but I didn't want to complicate this fishing expedition.

Besides, my budget wasn't that fat. Maybe I'd go home and write 'em a letter. I looked back at the elevator the couple had entered and noted that the cage had stopped on the eighth floor. It rested there just long enough for two people to exit, then it started down again.

"Anything you can tell me about Elite?"

"Nope. No calls, no admittance, no visitors."

"Do you know the people who work there?"

"No comment. Look, buddy, I've got things to do. You aren't getting up there so move it on out."

I shrugged. Maybe he didn't like my tennies. I told him thanks and started away, angling toward the elevators a little. When I looked back at the guard, he was watching but he didn't seem concerned. When I got closer I could see why. No lighted up or down buttons. Just a key slot. The whole building apparently had serious security concerns. Something to think about. I changed direction and headed for the revolving door I came in by. As I walked to my car, sitting in the late afternoon sun, a late model Audi sedan exited the underground parking ramp and turned left toward the freeway. It was beige.

Chapter 18

I spent the rest of the day and most of the next finding and eliminating more ice-blue late-model Audis. About four that afternoon I checked out the fifteenth owner on my list of possibles and then decided to pursue a different piece of this puzzle. Home again, home again, jiggery jog. I was going to see what I might learn about Don Molinaro's missing attendant. One Martin Levy.

The scorched leaves on the oak tree across the street had mostly fallen off and the bright yellow tape had been removed. All the debris had been swept up and carried off to wherever such debris is taken. My street was once again a serene quiet suburban scene, drowsing in the late afternoon summer heat. But who knew what passions boiled, what evil thoughts disturbed napping matrons behind their drawn shades, isolated by humming central air conditioning. Who knew what evil? . . . yeah. I didn't see any unknown vehicles, and I swung into my driveway with a faint smile on my face.

Inside, after I disabled the alarm system and put my fingers briefly on the shotgun in the closet, I went to the telephone. I'm not sure why I do that, touch the shotgun in the closet. Just to reassure myself, I guess. I had the instrument in my hand, the phone, that is, when I looked out the big picture window at the street. That was okay. The thing that stopped me was the window on the back side of the house. I was standing between two large windows, forming a silhouette from either side of the place. Sort of a sitting duck. I had no idea if the thug who was gunning for me knew where I lived. But I know a lot of people, and I know where they live. It isn't that hard to find someone who's not on the move constantly, who has roots in the community. I have roots. Shoot, I have a garden. So I pulled the shade on the window overlooking my back yard. Just in case. Bad stuff, I thought, being nervous about a shooter in my own home. I had to do something about it.

Martin Levy, aka a couple of aliases, was an intriguing puzzle. Except for the brief forays to the local gym, he appeared to have had no life of his own separate from Molinaro. Strange. That's real devotion. Maybe family? It occurred to me I'd started out the other day to visit the local muscle parlor and inquire about Mister Levy but hadn't got there. Now was the time.

It was only a five minute drive to a local mall and exercise heaven. Nervous or not, crick in my neck or not, I wasn't going to let the shooter turn me into a hermit. Fitness Fitness is a huge place, with a long row of stationary bicycles, a room of complex machines, racks of weights and treadmills. The machines were shiny chrome with black leather pads, more weights and other attachments on pegs around the walls. They looked as if they could be adapted to bondage or torture machines with a few twists and locks. And mirrors. Lots of mirrors on the wall.

I deduced from signs over the unoccupied reception desk that FF also offered massage, sauna, steam room and whirlpool. There must have been twenty or thirty people in the place when I got there. Sound whispered from a multiplicity of earphones hung around the main exercise room, attached to TV sets all tuned to the same news channel. It was a coed place with a clientele that seemed at my glance to vary from upper teen to upper thirties in age. Everybody in my view appeared to be in fine physical shape. The skin-tight spandex clothing they wore didn't hide much. Nobody appeared to be packing a weapon. I felt oddly overdressed. The place had a peculiar odor, a mixture of sweat, treated pool water and lubricant, probably used on the machines. Maybe for massages.

A slender young black man in a white tee and tan shorts appeared around a partition and smiled brightly at me. "Hiya," he said. "How can I help you?"

"I have information that a gentleman I must find may be a member here. He's come into some money, but his last address is incorrect. I wonder if you could help me?" I thought I saw a tiny gleam in the boy's eyes. Was that avarice, perhaps?

"Well, our membership lists are private. I'm afraid . . ." His voice trailed off and he stared at the folded twenty I was holding in my cupped palm.

"I expect Mr. Levy will be very grateful to whoever helps me put him in touch with the family." Yeah, right. I had a suspicion that this particular family, to which I suspected my large clients were attached, would likely blow Mr. Levy to kingdom come if I found him. I called him Levy as a calculated ploy. He might have used an alias, but I figured that since this place was so close to the retirement home there was a chance of his running into a staff person here so he would use the same name, or alias, that he used at the retirement place.

The young man looked at me for a long moment and then went behind the partition from which he had appeared. I hoped he was looking at the membership list. When he reappeared a few minutes later, he looked disappointed. I guess he figured if he didn't have any information for me, there'd be no reward.

"Anything?" I asked.

He shook his head. "The thing is, the manager isn't good about entering the names in the computer, so sometimes he misses people. I had a woman in here last week who said she'd been coming for years, almost every week. And I'm pretty sure I recognized her. But I couldn't find her name anywhere."

"Did she have a membership card?"

He shrugged. "Yeah but," he shrugged again, "sometimes they just come in and flash a card that looks right, and some people share a membership, you know?"

"All right, look," I said, not terribly interested in the club's management difficulties, "he had a tattoo of some kind of bird—"

"Green!" The kid nodded vigorously. "Sure, on his left arm. Runs all the way from his shoulder to his wrist. Sure, I remember him. Dark curly haired guy. He's been coming here off and on for a long time."

"But you don't have Martin Levy listed. What was this guy's name?"

Another shrug. "Don't remember."

Off to one side in the big exercise room I saw a flash of light. Then another. When I turned to look the kid said, "Pictures. Sometimes people like pictures of their workout buddies or of their improvement. You know. We have a gallery too." He pointed off to his left.

"Yeah? Show me," I said.

So he did. There was a long bulletin board hanging on the wall in a corridor that seemed to lead somewhere. On the board were about a hundred snapshots of posing and posturing denizens of the place, showing off their bodies and their muscles. On some of them somebody had scrawled a date or a note about weight loss or lifting strength. In a few, people in the background were going about their routines. There were too many to stand around and look at. Besides, the bulletin board was at normal height for normally sized people. I couldn't reach the top two or three rows without a stool or a chair.

"Do me a favor, kid," I said. I raised one eyebrow, ala Bogart. "Go through your pictures for me and see if you can find a snap of this Levy fellow, the man with the bird on his arm. There'll be a small reward if you locate one. By the way, do you remember the last time he was in here?"

"On my shift, last week. That was the last time. Tuesday, probably. Of course, we're open long hours, so he coulda come in when I wasn't here."

I gave him my card with the phone number and no address. We shook hands and he palmed my folded twenty like a pro.

Chapter 19

Satisfied I'd at least started something, I drove home. I needed a picture of this guy, Levy. It was fortunate he had that bird tattoo on his arm otherwise this could be a long hunt. I decided to rest my bunions and do a little finger-walking.

The Revulon cousins had given me some basic instruction in using the computer to find people, so I started there. Mainly, the cousins had introduced me to various search engines and web sites. It was a time-consuming, mind-numbing effort. There were a million Levys on the Internet, and they all had stories to tell.

After an hour I called the Roseville PD. With my red Keds propped on my table and a cold beer in hand, I reached my good bud, Sergeant Helen Lasker. "So, Sarge, what's the latest word on the mad bomber of Roseville?"

"The odometer was a false trail. The chair manufacturer said that electric machines that are rented sometimes have a small odometer attached for billing and record-keeping purposes."

"This was a rented chair?"

"Not to Mr. Molinaro. He purchased the chair, or at least he paid for it. We think Levy actually picked it up. Apparently it had originally been set up for rental. BCA found evidence of a remote triggering device that was familiar, so they have some parameters. They also are pretty sure the trigger and bomb were recent additions to the chair."

"Which may mean something changed that caused somebody

to decide it might be time for Mr. Molinaro to be eliminated. I wonder what that could have been?"

"Long shot, Sean," said Helen. "I'm beginning to think there are so many dimensions and possibilities to this thing we may never figure it out."

"I'm not ready to give up just yet. What do we know about the trigger?"

"Radio freq apparently. Depending on what's around, the trigger had to be no more than a block away. A couple of hundred feet. Longer in open country, closer in an urban place."

"Concrete and steel can block the signal," I deduced.

"Exactly," Lasker agreed.

"Could have been somebody sitting in an Audi a block or so away, right? Or in the next block, maybe in the home's parking lot."

"Ahh, your mysterious Audi. Sure, Sean, or the bomb could have been set off by somebody in the living room of one of your neighbors."

"Doubt that. No new neighbors for quite a while. Anything else?"

"What have you got for me?"

"Fitness Fitness. It's the exercise place where Mr. Levy went occasionally for workouts. The one in the mall across from Rosedale. That's it from my end, although I'm getting a handle on the sale of ice-blue Audis."

"Okay. Thanks for the tip. We'll send somebody over." There was a pause. "Sean?"

"Yeah."

"How you doing?"

"Okay. I'm getting a crick in my neck from looking over my shoulder, though."

After we hung up the telephones, I decided the crick in my neck was a little more fact than fiction so I took myself to my

The Case of the Deceiving Don

basement. Nothing elaborate there. I have a cheap stationary bike and a pretty good rowing machine. I spent fifteen minutes on each and felt a lot better afterwards. I showered and decided a walk was on the agenda. Like I said, I'm not going to be a hermit. My career would flat out go in the tank if I just curled up in the house. Besides, outside I can maneuver, see more around me. Hear thugs sneaking up.

In old, ratty but clean work-in-the-yard clothes, a long-billed cap that effectively shielded my face, and an old pair of red Keds, I sauntered down the street and around the curve to the edge of Sheltering Limbs' property. I turned left along the paved walking path until I got beyond the first small hill and a grove of trees. Then I cut across the vast expanse of grass to the west, following the lumpy contours of the ground. Every twenty yards or so I took a long gander at the back of the home's main building. In an earlier life it had been a junior high school, so there were plenty of windows in the main building. I noted a door at one end beside an added building or shed that appeared to contain a large pile of sand. Probably for the walks and the parking lot in winter.

I couldn't see if there was another door in the common wall, but the building was completely open on the south side, so I thought not. Around on the west side of the place more windows on the upper two floors—the building only had three stories—some with curtains, some with drawn shades. I saw movement behind a couple of them. On the first floor, a lot of the windows were bricked over on the outside. I assumed some of the classrooms had been extensively remodeled into offices or living suites. According to my information, Don Molinaro had had a suite of two small bedrooms with a common sitting room between them on the first floor.

Midway along the west wall I saw a set of steps leading down to a door painted a contrasting dark green. I assumed it led to the basement level. Now I was approaching a private home behind an unpainted wooden fence about twelve feet high, first in a short row of three houses that lay along the property line of the retirement home. I could hear faint splashing and the happy sound of laughter. Kids in an outdoor pool, apparently. It was hot enough.

I had to cut to the west to get to the street beyond the houses. Now I was a block away, entering a cul de sac from between two private homes. There were grassy paths so I knew it was a common route. Nevertheless I picked up my pace, looked neither left or right. Just another walker out enjoying the heat. As I stepped onto the pavement, the hair on my neck prickled. I thought I'd come under the more-than-casual gaze of a vigilant homemaker. I casually glanced around. I thought I saw someone, maybe a woman looking my way from an upstairs window of the big split-level behind me. No one shouted at me. I didn't want anyone to call the cops on me so I got moving again. When I got to County Road D, a short block away from the retirement place, I turned right and went down the edge of the pavement in the bike lane. I angled across the parking lot of Sheltering Limbs. From there I counted two more doors, one at each end of the building. Both were set up to allow entrance with a minimum of fuss. The curbs were cut down for wheelchairs and people no longer able to lift their feet very high. I already knew there weren't any doors on the east wall. As I headed down the street on the east side, I noted that Director Tompkins's office was dark. Middle of the day. If he was just somewhere else in the building, the lights would still be on. They weren't, and I could see that the door was closed because there wasn't any light from the hall leaking in. He was gone, out of the building. Probably. I wondered why.

I turned around and headed back for the corner door where I already knew the reception desk was located. Inside, the long hallway beckoned. It was very quiet. The receptionist, a different one from my last visit, appeared from a small alcove behind her barrier, eyebrows raised in query.

Chapter 20

"I was just wondering. I mean, I know I don't have an appointment, but is the director available?"

"I'm sorry I believe he's already left for the day. Perhaps one of the staff could assist you?"

"Well, that might be a possibility. I am interested in this establishment and . . ." My mind was racing. I was vamping, dribbling out words, looking for a way to penetrate the veil of secrecy Tompkins had tried to maintain. I'd made a few rents in the fabric, but I wanted more. Always more. I scratched my head and tried to look thoughtful.

"Well it's about time!" The voice was just short of a screech. "You there! Young man, you're late." The voice came from a tiny figure in a wheelchair who had just appeared from down the hall and now came wheeling toward us at a furious rate.

"Oh, dear," murmured the receptionist. She raised her voice, "Now Blanche, you mustn't bother this gentleman."

I seized my opportunity, winking at the receptionist. "Aunt Blanche! Aunt Blanche," I called. "I didn't realize you were living here at Sheltering Limbs." I walked swiftly down the tiled hall, soles squeaking, toward the tiny figure in the wheelchair. She halted in what I suspected was startled consternation and looked like she was about to reverse direction.

"What? I'm not—"

I reached her and squatted to eye level. I smiled and gave her another big wink. "You remember me, Aunt Blanche. Don't you? I'm your nephew, Sean." I didn't want to get into any more family detail than necessary, figuring they could easily check her records if they got suspicious. If they did that, they might learn she had no local relative named Sean.

I almost held my breath, waiting for her reaction. The receptionist swished up and stopped just behind me. Blanche barely flicked the woman a glance. She looked pretty grim, but her wizened hand snaked out and clutched my wrist on the arm of her wheelchair. I felt her nails bite into my skin.

"Humph," she snorted. "You better come along with me. I haven't had a real family visit in weeks." She released my hand and spun the chair around. A faint smell of sour milk enveloped us. Without a backward glance she trundled off back the way she'd come.

"You can visit in the rec room until supper is served, Blanche." The receptionist turned and went back up the hall toward her post. I stood up and followed Blanche.

The rec room was across the hall and a few doors down from the director's office. I took a quick look at the doorknob as I went by. The rec room or lounge was a big room with a host of tables and chairs scattered about. There weren't any windows, but the lights were all on and it was very bright. Along one long wall was a series of cabinets, a Formica counter with more cabinet doors below. In the opposite corner from the door was a small sink. On the wall across from the cabinets was a big white bulletin board littered with announcements of various activities.

Blanche rolled across the room and banged into a table, where she stopped. The only other person in the room, an old bent man, looked up briefly from his examination of the table top where he was seated and then went back to his contemplation. The woman did a slow spin beside the table and squinted up at me. "Sit, boy," she said. "We have to talk." She pointed imperiously at a chair by the table. I sat.

"Well," she rasped. "You know my name. I'm Blanche Essen. A gentleman would reciprocate."

"Essen?" I smiled. "I was sort of hoping it was Dubois. My name is Sean Sean. I'm a private detective."

"Really! Are you here about Mr. Molinaro? Gus?"

"Why would you think that?"

"Listen, Sonny. I may be old and stuck in this contraption at this place, but I still have a wit or two about me. I heard you talking to Ellen. Sounded to me like you were trying to figure a way in here. Unless I'm way off base, you don't have a legit reason for being here. Am I right?"

"Well."

"So what do you think the Vikings' chances are to make the playoffs this year?"

"Excuse me?"

"Look, sonny. If I'm going to help you, and I can, you know, you have to do something for me, got it? A *quid pro quo* as it were."

"All right, Blanche. What's your last name again?"

"Essen. Not that it matters. There aren't any more of me. I only had the one boy, and he died many years ago."

"I'm sorry for your loss," I said.

"Don't be," she responded tartly. "We never had what you'd call a close relationship. Now you, shorty."

"I think the Vikings will make the playoffs, and they have a good chance to go all the way."

"Good. Why are you here?"

"Do you give everybody a nickname?" Blanche blinked and did a small double-take.

"Quick, aren't you. Short and quick. No. Only the people I get on with."

"Did you know Mr. Molinaro?"

"Slightly. He was pleasant but held things real close. He

The Case of the Deceiving Don

didn't gossip and whenever his keeper was around, he talked even less."

"You mean Martin Levy?"

"Levy was around a lot. He was protective."

"How would you describe their relationship? Levy and Molinaro?"

"Tight, but not real friendly. Look, sonny, most of the geezers in this place have their wits and enough money to indulge themselves if they stack up the energy. Don Molinaro had plenty of loot. I mean, his own personal guy, a two-room suite. I can tell you this place isn't cheap. So he had plenty of coin of the realm, know what I mean? Anyway, I usta play gin rummy with Gus—Mr. Molinaro."

"Wait a minute," I said. "A minute ago you called him Don. Which is it, Gus or Don?"

Blanche cocked her head at me. "Get me a bottle of water from the 'fridge, will you? I'm not real fond of what comes out of the fountain coolers around here." I did that.

When I returned she had me rip the plastic seal off then she grabbed the bottle and took a healthy swig. "Look," she said. "I may be old and half crippled up, but I keep up with things. By now you should know that Gus was connected. I bet he was a made man. Didn't you read *The Godfather?*" She peered up at me shrewdly. "Gus Molinaro was a don, a Mafia Don. Get it? So I figure he's either hiding out here or Levy is his minder or just a perk from the mob when he retired." Her eyes sparkled. She was having a good old time with me.

I smiled at Blanche. "How do you know all this?"

She winked again. "See this chair?" She smacked her palm on the contraption's arm rest. "I can get around a little, get into bed or a chair, go to the toilet. But I can't walk more'n a few steps at a time. We got groups here, cliques. I'm a wheelie. Those that walk don't hang around us so much. I guess it hurts too much to bend over to talk with us." She shrugged. "Doesn't matter. So those of us in chairs tend to hang together more. Another wheelie has a computer, and he does a lot of searching and finding stuff. One day he found this web site about the Mafia, you know, the mob? And Gus's name was in it.

"Now Gus, he played pretty good gin rummy, and I taught him to play whist. Martin Levy, he was no card player. Gus and I talked a little when we played. I asked him if he knew anything about the Mafia. He denied it, of course. He told me he'd always had to live with the accident of having the same name as some guy in the Mafia. Some here believe him; some don't. But there's a lot of talk, you know. Most of us got too much time on our hands and too little to do besides talk." She grinned and I saw she was missing a couple of teeth. "You'd call it gossip."

"So tell me, Blanche. How come you and I connected here?"

"That's easy. I overheard some of the staff talking about this cute detective who came around to talk to the director and some others about Mr. Molinaro. That was you, buster. When I heard you talking to the receptionist just now, I just wheeled on out to see if you were the one."

"Okay. Whaddaya know?"

"Just like that?"

"Sure. We'll talk about what I can do for you after."

She squinted at me. "After? Can I trust you?"

"I haven't stiffed anybody yet, far as I know."

Blanche put her hand in front of her mouth and grinned. "You sound like a guy out of the forties. How long you been doing this?"

"Being a private investigator?" Blanche nodded. "About six years on my own. Before that I worked for an outfit in South Saint Paul."

"How come I never heard of you?"

The Case of the Deceiving Don

"Well, isn't that the idea? That's what being private means, doesn't it?"

She nodded and grinned at me again, this time letting her bad teeth show. "When do you answer my questions?"

"You noticed, right? Later, maybe. If you don't get too impertinent. So what can you tell me about Augustus Molinaro and his man, Mr. Martin Levy?"

Most of what she could tell me I already had, although I would have known it sooner if Blanche and I had connected earlier. Her story confirmed what I knew about Molinaro. I didn't tell her I already had most of her facts. She gave me one intriguing piece of information. Tompkins seemed to spend more than ordinary amounts of time in conversation with Levy.

"One night, this woulda been about three weeks ago, very late at night. See, I get insomnia some times. When that happens, sometimes I read and sometimes I listen to the radio. Sometimes I just get into my wheels and wander the halls. Once in a while I hook up with someone who's also up. We play a little gin, or double sol, you know.

"It's sort of frowned on, even if we're supposed to be able to come and go as we please. But the night staff doesn't mind much if I don't bug the other guests. Anyway, on that night in question, I saw light in Tompkins' office, and I rolled on up there. The door was part-way open, and I could hear Tompkins talking first on the phone and then with Levy. I know it was Levy 'cause after while he came out and went away down the hall to his room."

"Did he see you?"

"No, I didn't talk to him, I just watched him go."

I considered that. I thought it was a good thing she hadn't been noticed.

"Did you hear what they were saying?"

She shook her head. "Nope, just that they both sounded

tense. Agitated, you might say."

I thought it was also a good thing that she hadn't overhead their conversation in any detail.

Chapter 21

The next morning, three days after Augustus Molinaro met his maker, I was back at Fitness Fitness in our local shopping mall. This time I had a picture. It wasn't a very good one. Blanche had remembered some snaps on the bulletin board from a big picnic the inmates had had in Como Park some weeks ago. Of course, Gus Molinaro and his shadow, Martin Levy had been there. So she showed me the pictures and there, in the background, not in very sharp focus, was my target, Martin Levy, standing beside Don Molinaro. I'd borrowed the photo, made a late night visit to a friend of mine with considerable talent and his own darkroom. In a few hours he'd produced an acceptable print that isolated Levy.

I'd vetted the print by showing it to the receptionist at Sheltering Limbs. She recognized Levy right off. When I laid it on the counter at the fitness place, the guy glanced at it and said, "Sure, Mel Larson. He's a member. Haven't seen him in several days, though. Ever since I can remember, three, four years anyway, he's been coming, mostly in the mornings. 'Course, he might have changed times."

"What did he do here?"

"Pretty standard. He'd come in, go change at his locker, do a routine on the machines, shower and leave. He wasn't very sociable. Didn't talk much."

"Did he have a regular locker?"

"No. We don't rent lockers. You come in, pick up a towel,

grab whatever one is available. The keys stay in the door when they're open, you know?"

I nodded. "Okay. Thanks." Outside, I slipped the photo of Levy into the envelope and headed for the car. I figured there wasn't much use in talking to other people in the shopping center. It sounded like Levy had only minimal contact with people around him. No lingering, no window shopping. Whether by accident or design, I didn't know yet.

I headed to the office. I didn't see any silver or ice-blue late-model Audis, and you can bet I was watching. Nor did I notice anyone with a rifle on the streets I passed. My office was undisturbed when I entered. I clicked on the air conditioning to get rid of the hot musty smell and skimmed through the mail. As usual, it wasn't much. A couple of bills, several pieces of advertising, and a welcome check from an insurance company I'd done a small task for.

There was one advertising piece I read all the way through. At first I thought it might be something I could use. It was an ad for a new type of body armor. It seemed like something a riot squad might want. Supposedly the armor would stop anything up to a .50 caliber machine gun slug. When I looked more closely at the description it appeared unwieldy and heavy enough to anchor me to the ground in a small tornado. Thanks but no thanks.

I sauntered on down the hall to the Revulon cousins' place of business. The door was locked but I could see light on behind the door glass. A small hand lettered sign said Please Knock. So I did that. "Who's there?" came a squeaky voice from a tiny speaker that I could see was temporarily attached to the wall beside the door.

"The boogie man," I responded.

"We have no need of boogies, this morning, sorry."

"It's Sean. What's the deal?"

The Case of the Deceiving Don

The door chattered at me, and I turned the knob. Inside things were the same scene as always, except for the intercom box at Belinda's workstation. "Good morning," I said. "Has something happened? Are you getting paranoid?"

Betsey appeared from the other room where the noisier and larger machines of their trade were stashed. She was wearing a dark blue tank top that emphasized her considerable cleavage and tight white slacks that called attention to her hips and bottom. She grinned wide-lipped at me. "We have a new contract. It requires an upgraded level of security. So the electric door lock and intercom were added yesterday."

I looked where she pointed at the door. It was one of those standard 1940's style office jobs with a big pebbled-glass window in it. Betsey saw me looking at the door and nodded, "They're coming to put up bars on the window this afternoon. And look at this." She pointed.

In the corner under the window that looked out at the parking lot was a big new beige machine.

"It's our new super-fast shredder. Watch." She fed a sheet of paper in one end. The big beige machine snatched the paper out of her hand and hummed for a second. Strips of paper fell into a bag under the machine.

I nodded, impressed, and glanced out the window. At the edge of the lot, partway into the alley was a late model ice-blue Audi.

"Shit," I muttered and ran back to my office. I grabbed my .38 Chief's Lightweight from the safe and ran down the stairs. But when I burst out of the rear door into the lot, the Audi was nowhere to be seen. I ran around the building to Central and just caught a glimpse of what could have been the same vehicle going down Central toward the center of the city.

I bolted to my car and tore out of the lot, just missing getting creamed by a citizen in an old Buick who happened by. His mouth was moving as he apparently screamed at me through the windshield, but I couldn't hear him. I made it to the Third Avenue Bridge over the big Mississippi, anxiously scanning the vehicles ahead. I wanted to catch the car, but I didn't want to overrun it. If it was the right one, I didn't want to tip my hand that I was on to them. If I was. Just as we exited the bridge beside the yellow US Post Office building, I saw the object of my desire three cars ahead of me. Another block and the vehicle pulled to the curb. A suit got out. The car pulled away, and I followed. Just as we turned the corner onto Washington, I looked to my right and there was the suit, trotting up the steps to the marble Federal Building. Lot of federal offices in that building, including the CIA, the FBI, the DEA and some other alphabets.

I followed the Audi down Washington and onto the freeway. Eventually we exited in Edina, and the dog I was tailing wagged us right to a private underground parking location. It was under an office building I recognized right off. I'd been there before when I wanted to talk to someone in the Elite Corporation. The one with no visitors, no admittance, no calls. Well, well. Circumstantial? You bet, but good enough for me. I was definitely on the right trail.

On the way back north I took a small detour to a neighborhood coffee shop and diner in south Minneapolis just off the strip. I knew one of the owners slightly. Ann Gross was working the counter as usual, just as she had been the day I met her. Ann and I got to know each other last year when I'd been in the neighborhood, waiting for a guy thought to be scamming his insurance company to come home. When I walked in out of the crisp sunny fall afternoon that day, a man sitting at the counter was yelling at the woman behind the counter. He was getting belligerent and almost physical with the waitress, who turned out to be Ann. As I walked up, she gestured with one hand. By pure accident she knocked the coffee cup, and its hot contents into his lap. When he stood up screaming, I somehow tripped and tangled my legs with his. When we went down in a heap wouldn't you know, I landed right on his chest with my elbow deep in his belly. Took the wind right out of him, poor fellow. Of course I apologized profusely and even offered to pay his dry cleaning bill, but by then he just wanted to get as far away from Ann and me as he could and that meant gone from that diner. Tsk.

I looked at Ann, and she looked back. She thanked me, but it was pretty clear she thought she had the situation taken care of before I interfered. She probably did, but being of the old school, I had leapt in before it was necessary.

I acknowledged that, had a chuckle, a cuppa, and a nice slice of their fresh banana cream pie with heaps of whipped cream, a little gossip with Ann, and then I went back to the office.

This time she smiled and nodded when I came through the door. I slid onto a stool and like magic, a steaming cup of black coffee appeared before me.

Chapter 22

Back in my office I considered what I had learned. My former boss, Duke Fararra, the owner of the agency where I'd trained to be a P.I., taught me that sometimes you had to kick the tires to dislodge the rust. I was going to do that, metaphorically. On the main floor of my building was a small print shop where one could do some typing and mailing. I used an old portable typewriter they had lying around to compose a brief letter in which I explained I had some information the letter's recipient needed. For a fee, I'd provide it. The information I had.

I could have done the letter on my computer, but I wasn't good with it for things like this. Besides, I wanted a deliberately low-tech appearance. I typed that the information was about the recently dead Augustus Molinaro. I suggested they call my representative, detective Sean Sean, and I put in my office telephone number.

I signed it, Martin Levy.

I addressed it to the Elite Agency in Edina.

I didn't wear gloves, and I didn't care about other traces I might leave since I just wanted to see if I could break something loose. Rattle a cage or two, so to speak. Elite knew where my office was, and they knew where I lived. So I mailed the letter and went home.

The next morning, after a peaceful night with my cats, a delicious steak and baked potato, and Yo Yo Ma on the stereo, I sat down at my home computer, a nice, state of the art Dell, and

The Case of the Deceiving Don

Googled up Mr. Augustus Molinaro. I spent a couple of hours wandering the Internet dipping into various government and media sites, collecting bits and pieces on Don Molinaro. Some of this research had been done before and by others. But I was looking with a different eye. I wasn't just collecting information, I was looking for clues. I was searching for something like a loose thread I could pluck out of the fabric of this event.

What I assembled gave me some clues as to what might be going on. Molinaro came out of a Boston family. He spent some time in New York and then went off to Pennsylvania. I got the impression he was kind of a visiting fireman, or maybe a trusted liaison. In any case, he settled down in Mechanicsburg where he then rose steadily through the ranks to become a kingpin of the Eastern Pennsylvania Mafia.

Mechanicsburg is a small place, essentially a western suburb of Harrisburg in east-central Pennsylvania. It's on the Susquehanna River. Which wanders through the Tuscarora and Appalachian mountains on its way to Chesapeake Bay. Pretty country out that way. Why is it important? If you drive north along the river a few hours you come up to Milton. It's an easy scenic sort of drive with the White Deer Ridge rising ahead. You'll see signs for the town of White Deer and another place called Allenwood.

Allenwood has seen a lot of mobsters and other assorted criminals over the years. It's the site of a large federal prison complex. One of the biggest in the federal prison system. So Mechanicsburg isn't such a bad place to be headquartered if you function as a kind of inside/outside liaison. And you might acquire a lot of juicy secrets. And if you were a careful Don Augustus Molinaro—greasy Gus—after a while you might just become a liability. Or not.

I was going to find out, hopefully not by traveling to Pennsylvania. There was a surprising amount of information, both official and not so official, about Allenwood on the Internet. There wasn't a floor plan of course, and the maps were a little short on exactitude. So I called the Bureau of Prisons. Yes, under certain guidelines and under the rules for particular prisoners, almost anyone could visit almost any prisoner. If said prisoner agreed.

Now, in spite of what they tell you about security, information flows back and forth. So does contraband. I was getting an idea that just maybe Don Molinaro was targeted for past actions or indiscretions which may have only come to light in recent times. If that were true, knowing what changes had occurred could lead me to the why of the bomb. From there it could be an easy step to the who of it. So the question of the moment became what sorts of information and other illegal goods might the good Don have been handling? I would find out.

I went to my office and checked the roof across the street. It was empty. I checked the street. No ice-blue late model Audis in sight. I ran my new blinds up and down a couple of times. Nice and smooth. The telephone rang.

It was my cop friend, Ricardo Simon. "How's tricks, dude?" he asked.

"Okay. I'm still a little jumpy, as you can imagine. Any information for me?"

"Not on the Molinaro thing. I'm calling because we got a notification that Mrs. Higgins has been released."

"What, probation?"

"Yeah. Good behavior. Thought you'd want to know."

"I appreciate the heads up, but I didn't take her daughter's threat seriously, did you?"

"Nope. Just wanted you to know," he said.

"Is she staying in town?"

"Oh, sure. Her listed address is their place on the south side."

"Thanks. Let's have dinner one day."

"On you. Take care, Sean." Simon hung up the phone.

Mrs. Higgins. Huh. I'd been instrumental in getting her put away back a couple of years. She'd had an accident on the job at some insurance company. Figured she knew enough to stiff the company for a whole lot of money. Nice older lady, until you got in her way. Then she could turn nasty. I followed her around for a while and discovered her back and hip problems weren't anywhere near as bad as she and her doctor said they were. I'd testified in court that my pictures and video of her cavorting in the water at Hidden Lake were true and unedited. I guess it didn't help that she wasn't wearing any clothes. Anyway, when the jury convicted her, she stood up in court and called me some names in most unfortunate language, concluding as the bailiffs muffled her that she'd get me.

I hung up and went to the bathroom. When I got back to my office, the message light was blinking so I played the recording. There was only one call, from Blanche at the retirement home. "Hey, sonny," she said. "Good recording on your answer machine. Get your buns out here as soon as you can. I got some intelligence for you."

Uh oh. If these imperative calls became a frequent pattern, Blanche could get to be a nuisance. On the other hand, she might have something significant for me. I decided to compromise with myself. I'd go over to Sheltering Limbs tomorrow morning on my way into the city from home, instead of right now.

That turned out all right. But Blanche seemed to have figured it out. She was grinning when I showed up in the visitors lounge at ten the next morning.

"That's right. Take your time, sonny. If you'd been here yesti-day, you mighta been able to take advantage of what I got to tell you. As it is, you'll have to wait now."

"Good morning, Blanche," I said, sitting down beside her. "Why are you sitting over here?" She'd wedged her chair into a corner beside a potted mock corn plant and a long sofa. She was facing the door with the wall of windows on her left. A game of solitaire was spread out on the table in front of her.

She gave a vigorous shake to her gray head and riffled the cards with still nimble fingers. "Gotta watch my back, sonny. Didn't you ever read about Wild Bill? Only time he forgot to sit with his back to a wall he got shot in the head from a window behind him. Holding the dead man's hand, right?"

"A what?"

"Dead man's hand. Aces and eights."

"I'm afraid my education is lacking in that area. You want to make that clearer?"

She sighed in what I took to be mild exasperation. "You play poker, sonny?"

"Nope."

"Wild Bill was killed during a poker game in Deadwood, South Dakota. He was holding two black pair. Aces and eights. The dead man's hand." Blanche smirked at me.

"Aren't there five or seven cards in a poker hand?"

"They would have been playing draw poker. Five cards to a hand."

"Is this why you called me, Blanche? What was the fifth card?"

"Dunno. Nobody knows for sure what the last card was." She smiled and glanced around although the room was still empty. "Gus and that Levy fellow are one pair. Your clients are another pair."

I didn't remember saying anything about clients, plural, to Blanche. In fact, I didn't remember telling her anything about this case. Let it go for the moment, I thought. Bad decision.

"All right, who's the fifth card in this analogy of yours?"

The Case of the Deceiving Don

"Tompkins. He's a wild card."

"Tompkins? Why?" I was interested in her reasons, because I'd already tagged him as somebody more involved in this business than it appeared on the surface. Not because of his reticence over affairs of his charges; that was legitimate. There was just something about the guy that set off warning bells.

"He's the man you gotta concentrate on. If you'da showed yesterday, he was gone all day. In Chicago for a meeting. Might be there's some info in his office. Now you'll have to wait for another time."

I leaned forward until we were almost nose to nose. "Now you listen here, Blanche Essen. Stay the hell away from him. I don't want to hear about some midnight wheelies in his office, you hear? I mean it. I'm interested in what you hear and see, but let's have no early morning prowling. Got it? No B&E stuff."

Blanche looked affronted. "Of course not, sonny. Do I look stupid? You be my legs. I'm not much good for running anymore. Say, you got a bookie you can recommend?"

"Why?"

She shrugged. "No pa'tic'lar reason. I just might want to get a bet down on a baseball game. The Twins are looking pretty good right about now."

"That kind of gambling is illegal in Minnesota, you know," I said primly. She cackled. I patted the back of her wrinkled hand where it lay on the card table, and I rose to leave. I got an elaborate wink and walked out of the room. The receptionist smiled sweetly at me. "So nice of you to visit Blanche. She's lonely, poor soul. Doesn't get any other visitors since her grandson moved to California after her husband died."

Blanche was right. Tompkins did deserve some attention. I found it difficult, though not impossible, to believe that he was unaware of Molinaro's past associations. It's hard, over a lengthy period of ten years, say, to avoid making the occasional slip of the tongue, of revealing some bit of information about one's past. Information which might not be significant by itself but when put together with other bits collected over a period of time, say that same ten years, could reveal all sorts of background. And who would keep track of such bits and pieces?

Why, Mr. Tompkins, the fifteen-year head of Sheltering Limbs. Who else? Perhaps he had files on some of his inmate—er guests. Never above a little dark of the night reconnoitering, I considered the possibility of burgling Tompkins's office. It was a special problem. Because of its role as a shelter of the aging and the aged, and because it was certainly a high-end retirement home, it had a well-trained staff. At least I assumed so. Hadn't interviewed more than a couple of them, but the maintenance engineer, that Willard Johnson fellow, seemed pretty bright, and the couple of nurses. Even the sweet receptionist. The rules say residents of these establishments are supposed to have complete freedom, just the way they would at home. That's what the rules say. The facts are sometimes not so loose.

Chapter 23

A place like Sheltering Limbs had a night staff. I'm pretty good with locks and such, and being short and slim made it somewhat easier to slide in and out of places I shouldn't be. But even a reduced staff of wide-awake folks was a complication. Then there were the residents. Some of them were bound to be insomniacs. Blanche had mentioned that she was sometimes up at night, wheeling silently along the spectral halls like some other-worldly wraith. I wondered if she could do real wheelies in that chair. All elements I had to consider while paying greater attention to the smooth director of this establishment.

Blanche's insistence that the director's office might be an important source of information impelled me on and I determined that as a tenacious detective, I was going to penetrate Director Tompkins's sanctum and find out what was so important that he kept most of his files locked. How did I already know some of his files were locked? Easy. Observation. I'd looked around his office the one time I was visiting him, and lo and behold, some files in the long bank of cabinets were locked and some weren't. Of course, there were many rational and innocent reasons for locking things up. Personnel files, budget and payroll info. Tompkins could be an anal retentive security freak. I was going to find all that out. I hoped. Undetected, I hoped. B&E was not legal.

It was midnight on a moonless night. Not even a cloud, so the sky was black except for the stars. There wasn't the lightest breeze. It was cool, and there was a faint smell of rain in the air. Don't you just love it? A perfect night for skulking about. I donned black Lee jeans, black socks and for once eschewed my usual red tennies with the white soles. Instead I chose a pair of ancient black pumps with soft black rubber soles. They were so thin I could feel every pebble underfoot.

I also had a long-sleeved loose cotton pullover that was dyed midnight blue. From Lands End Outlet, I think. A second, so it was not expensive. I strapped on a well-padded fanny pack into which I had placed my lock pick set, an ordinary Craftsman double-ended screwdriver, a small flashlight and a pair of latex gloves. On my head I set my black long-billed fisherman's cap. I checked myself out in the mirror. I looked good. I was ready. I was also psyched.

Going to the front door, I was aware that my breathing was coming in a tight shallow rhythm and my heartbeat was elevated. I left my wallet and my house key on the desk, slipped the lock on the front door, and hiked on out. Jogging down the street and around the curve toward my target, I considered my alternatives. There were a couple of lights on in houses of my neighbors, but the block was quiet except for an occasional rustle of sleeping birds, disturbed as I wafted by. Most of the doors I'd passed on my earlier visits to the home were of the heavy fire-door security type that opened from inside with a panic bar. Almost impossible to breach without a key or explosives.

I knew I could get through the office windows most anywhere along the ground floor—I hadn't seen any tape or other intruder warning system. But for the most part they were high and exposed with no bushes around. I'd have to stretch to reach them and make like a scared rabbit every time somebody drove by. Besides on the street side where the windows were easiest to reach, there was the problem of streetlights.

There was one attractive possibility. On the west side of the building was that old door leading to the basement level. I'd seen it when I reconnoitered around the place. Plus it appeared from my casual-appearing glance to be painted wood rather than steel. I'd try that first.

I made a wide circle around the back of Sheltering Limbs. I heard the rumble of heavy-duty air conditioning, which pleased me. Outside noise would cover any B&E sounds I made. Moving closer I was screened from all but one or two upstairs windows of the neighboring houses. They were all dark. After watching and listening for a couple of minutes, I crept down the short outside stair to the door. Crouching there, I was almost invisible to any passing strollers. The darkness was pretty near absolute. No sky light penetrated the shadow of the building. I slipped on a latex glove and began to feel around. After almost getting a splinter in my thumb, I found the handle. My observations had been accurate and although it had two deadbolt locks, it only took me fifteen minutes to get them open. And I hardly damaged the door jamb at all. Recently oiled, the door squeaked nary a bit as I slid inside.

A musty tangle of odors greeted me. My halogen pencil light revealed I was in a large storage room nearly filled with stuff. There was furniture piled here and there and several tall shelf units holding boxes and smaller items. A broken desk lamp, an unbroken one and many boxes. Paper files of some kind. Gave me pause. Maybe I should look. Then I figured anything sensitive wouldn't be stored down here in this dust-choked musty place.

One door opposite me. I relocked the outside door with a single deadbolt. It snicked nicely into place.

The inside door facing me had a push-button knob lock. It didn't squeak either. Nor did the hinges. The hall was dark except for the occasional dim night light. My pumps whispered eerily as I scuttled down the hall to the south side of the place. Thankfully, the tile floor and my soles were compatible so I didn't squeak. I crept like a wraith along the hall to the stairs at the opposite end of the building.

Upstairs I was confronted with that long tiled hallway leading past the staff offices on my right and recreation rooms on the left. Just as I remembered. Mixed aromas came to me as I crouched there watching and listening. The smell of medicines, of bodies, of the wax and cleaners from the floor only a few inches below my nose. The passage was empty and better lit than the basement I'd just exited. Between the receptionist desk a hundred feet away, and me, there was nowhere to hide. Zero. The night duty nurse moved and adjusted something on her desk. I assumed it was female, it wasn't that easy to tell. When she sat still, I couldn't really see her. I conjured up an image of my previous visit when I'd talked with Tompkins. His office was five doors from the front of the place, but how many from this stairwell? I started crawling on my hands and knees up the hall, staying pressed against the office side. The image of the doors came to me then. I passed three, each recessed two or three inches. No hiding places.

The fourth door was Tompkins's. No light showed anywhere, except the dim glow from the recreation or common room a few steps away and from the front desk. I fished out my lock pick, leaned against the door on my knees, and went to work. Tompkins had a surprisingly good lock on his door. When the bolt finally snapped back, it sounded like a gun shot. I froze with my gloved hand on the door handle. The receptionist stood up and stretched. If she was going to the bathroom, she'd walk right toward me for a dozen steps. I was busted. Almost.

I clutched the door handle, unlatched it, and the door swung in, carrying me with it. I slid inside and slowly pushed the door back until there was just the tiniest crack through which I could eyeball the receptionist sauntering slowly toward me. With no hesitation she turned right and went into the facility. I exhaled and shut the door, locking it. For a minute or two, I wasn't sure, I just squatted there on the cool tile floor of the office. My heart rate slowed to something near normal. Time was a wasting so I crawled to the bank of file cabinets. Light flashed across the room. It was the headlights on a passing car.

Chapter 24

I stuck my tiny black maglight into my mouth so both hands were free and crawled to the row of file cabinets. I figured as long as I wasn't using much light, no one across the street would see me, but I was taking no chances. B&E was a crime, after all, and I didn't want to go to jail. There was too much to do. I could close the blinds, but there was always the possibility that some nosey parker would remember that a couple of hours ago they were open and call a cop.

There were a lot of four-drawer file cabinets, and I hoped I wouldn't be going into all of them. I'd still be there when Tompkins arrived for work that day, an embarrassing situation. I decided to focus on the locked cabinets, figuring they'd be more likely to contain sensitive information. There were five that were locked. Fortunately, the two closest to the windows were both unlocked. I carefully jimmied the others and a cursory look revealed the usual files, personnel records for the staff, medical and other records of the residents, some corporate files that I'd have liked to examine closely, but figured I didn't have the time. I scanned the staff files, but nothing leaped out at me. There was nothing hiding under the pendaflex files. It all appeared depressingly normal. Tompkins might have been hiding something in the unlocked file cabinets but my instinct said no. In our brief interview his facial expressions and body language had led me to believe that he was a secretive sort.

Either Tompkins was slyer than I figured or his sensitive stuff was somewhere else. The third possibility, that he had no sensitive stuff, I refused to consider. The first two cabinets were filled with files on various aspects of the operation. Just what was advertised on the drawer labels. Neat, alphabetically arranged hanging files. I checked all eight drawers, just to be safe. Unless he was hiding paper in files under phony names, I'd have nothing to show for my efforts. Then I made one interesting discovery.

In a drawer, tucked at the very back, was a wooden box. In the box was a .32 cal. blue-steel semi-automatic Smith and Wesson, an extra clip, and a box of bullets. Maybe Tompkins was worried about an attack by a crowd of maddened octogenarians. I left it where I found it. Many of the file drawers were empty or held little paper. That helped, but not much. I hadn't been sure what I hoped to find, something in the personnel files. It wasn't there. So I turned to the man's desk.

At that moment, the door handle to Tompkins's office twitched. I heard it before I saw it. Someone was trying the handle. All the doors in the place had levers, not knobs, as an accommodation to the elderly residents. I stopped breathing and peered across the desk at the door from my crouching position. There was just enough light so I could see the handle moving down and up, down and up. Hells Bells! I'd locked the door when I made entrance. Now I wondered who else might be making a late night foray into the director's private sanctum. My mind raced with possible solutions if whoever was out there had a key. I could take a header through a window. I could attack the innocent person as they came through the door and try to make a getaway down the hall to the basement. I could cower under the desk and hope I wasn't seen. Nuts. Who was out there, still trying the lever? I never found out. Maybe it was the night maintenance person making a cursory security check. Maybe I'd made a noise that attracted the receptionist.

After a minute the lever action stopped, and I slid across the floor to the door. Pressing my ear against the cool wood I heard soft footsteps receding. Sweat dripped off my nose. Temporary relief washed through my body. My attention was drawn to lights slowly traveling down the street outside the office. I scuttled to the window and peered out through the lowered blinds. Damn. Beset on all sides. Why was that car cruising by so slowly? The angle of the light wasn't right for me to see the color, but it could have been an Audi. On the other hand, I might be seeing figments. Without changing speed, the vehicle went around the bend onto Brenner and disappeared. I went back to the desk, which was locked.

This was a seriously upscale desk with a serious lock. Fortunately, it was the kind of executive desk with only a single serious lock, so once breached, all the goodies inside became mine. It had the kind of lock my lock picks were designed for so it was the work of only moments to open. I was becoming increasingly aware of the passage of time. The longer I tarried, the more likely I'd be discovered. It was now or never, to coin a phrase.

I rifled through the files. Nothing. I pawed through the lap drawer and then yanked on the bottom drawer in the other pedestal. It didn't want to slide out. I pulled harder and finally an envelope that had popped up to jam against the bottom of the drawer above gave it up. In the envelope was an unmarked diskette. A floppy, as they're known. Now what? It could be nothing. It could be Tompkins's private stash of porn. It could be his kid's birthday party. Did he have kids?

There wasn't a computer in the office but there was a dock. So I knew he must have had a portable that he carried around with him. I didn't want to leave without knowing something about the contents of the disk since it was the only thing I'd found of any interest at all. I was reluctant to leave knowing

The Case of the Deceiving Don

almost less than I came in with. I crouched there on the floor half in the kneehole of the desk and switched on my little Maglight. I examined the envelope. It was dusty and had been taped to something. That was interesting. I reached into the drawer and my questing fingers found some faint gravelly-like residue on the bottom of the drawer above. I rubbed my fingers together. Sticky residue. The envelope had apparently been taped to the bottom of the second drawer and the tape had given it up. It was thin enough that it nestled nicely between the drawer runners, but when the tape gave up, the envelope fell slightly and I found it. Hah.

No more thinking, no more pondering. I stuffed the envelope in my shirt pocket, collected my gloves and closed up shop. I had to leave the desk unlocked which was a problem if Tompkins discovered the missing disk before I could replace it. If that happened, I'd just figure something out. Now to make my exit.

I risked a look out the window. Over the houses across the street, I could see the black sky which seemed to have a touch of gray now. As I stared, a light came on in a bedroom directly across from me. Great. The neighborhood was astir. I padded softly across the floor and unlatched the door. It swung open with nary a sound. I lay down on the floor and slid my head around the jam until I should have been able to see the reception desk. Imagine my surprise when I found my nose engaging in a close encounter with a black plastic wastebasket. Somebody had come by and set it there. I assumed it was the same person who had tried the door earlier. That somebody was likely to come back in a few minutes to open the office door since I also assumed Director Tompkins didn't haul around his own waste bin.

Definitely time to go. Kneeling, I scanned the dim hallway. Nobody, and in fact there wasn't anybody at the front desk. I scooted out and closed the door not bothering to lock it. If

Tompkins or anybody else wondered about that, I figured those questions would remain forever unanswered. I hoped.

I made it to the corner and down the hallway past many doors to the stairs going down. Still dark. Still quiet. Like the ghost I was pretending to be I skipped noiselessly into the basement and retraced my steps to the storeroom. After that, my breathing scaled down and I relaxed, making sure I could lock the outside door. We didn't want any denizens of the night prowling around and disturbing the residents. I stripped off my latex gloves and wiped my sweaty palms on my thighs as I walked home.

The sun was definitely making its presence known in the east as I disarmed my alarm system and entered my dark house. I was impatient to see what was on my purloined disk but my adrenalin was leaking out and weariness swept over me. I dropped envelope, clothes, and body onto the bed. Everything would wait for a few hours. I needed some serious sack time.

Chapter 25

The sun was at its zenith when I awoke. I'd remembered to kill the telephone ringer, so when I wandered blearily down to the kitchen to whip up some coffee, I saw the blinking message light on the answering machine there on the table by the door. That meant one or more messages. If the light blinked rapidly, the messages had already been accessed. I suppose that was so you could tell if someone else had listened to your private messages. Who cared. I had no idea what a steady red glow meant because I hadn't read the instruction book.

I ignored the machine and went to the kitchen where I was able to cobble together some coffee and some cold water into a machine labeled coffee maker. While I waited for the machine to do its thing, I checked out my refrigerator and discovered I had the makings for scrambled eggs and bacon. Very good. No bread for toast. Sad. But, if one didn't go to the grocery store, one ran out of things. The way of the world.

Slumped at the dining room table I ate and drank. The eggs and the bacon, which didn't taste too old, filled the void in my belly, and the caffeine woke me up, at least partially. I retrieved the purloined disk, which had no identifying label, and stuck it in my computer. Wonder of wonders, it wasn't protected or encrypted or set to self-destruct without some arcane instructional sequence. Well, there was a code of sorts. Part of each entry was incomprehensible to my questing eye. I had an answer for that.

After peering at the screen for several minutes whilst slurping more hot coffee, I determined that what I apparently had was a record of money transfers, mostly incoming, some outgoing, over the past several years. Ten years to be more exact. The earliest dates coincided with the month after Director Tompkins had been installed at Sheltering Limbs. There appeared to be a regular monthly payment of five grand. Occasionally there would be a withdrawal, or at least that's what I deduced. The withdrawals left Tompkins with something like three quarters of a mil. A tidy sum on top of his regular salary. Because there weren't any dollar signs, just boxes and numbers, I was making some assumptions. It looked to me like I had a spread sheet. On the left was a column of numbers that could have been dates, then another box with a string of numbers that made no sense at all that I could see. Then another column of numbers which looked like amounts of money, large chunks of money.

My nature in these matters being basically suspicious, I assumed I was looking at cash flow. No way was this money that had a paper trail. Which naturally raised a question. Where was all this cash, these Franklins and Hamiltons and Lincolns? Not many Abes, I'd bet. Too bulky. In sealed jars under the back yard? In grocery bags in the back closet? How about a safe deposit box at some bank? Even that was problematic. Banks require records, signatures. And if the owner had to decamp in a hurry, in the dark of the moon say, said bank might not be open.

If it were me, I'd have moved the cash to several secure places far enough away that I could get to in a panic circumstance without setting off the alarms. On the other hand, maybe Director Tompkins just piled the stuff in a safe in his basement. Some people might suggest that I'm jumping to conclusions here. Well, that's what I do. I'm a P.I. I jump, and then I investigate. I follow leads, examine clues. Here was a lead, but I had no clue at the moment where it might lead.

I noted that the incoming payment entries were made on the fifth of every month. Meticulous, this guy. The last entry had been made only three days ago. That could mean I probably had almost thirty days to replace the disk before Tompkins discovered it missing. Good.

I dressed, laced up a clean pair of red Keds with the white laces and white soles. I drank more coffee, made a grocery list, and copied the disk to my own computer. I checked the answering machine—nothing interesting or relevant to my life—and headed out. Since the disk I'd stolen had nothing on it to identify it I penned a small dot in the corner of the blank label on it and tossed the diskette into a drawer with a bunch of others, some labeled, some not. Hiding in plain sight I called it.

I thought about what I had. First I had a blown up, apparently retired, mob guy, Augustus Molinaro. Then I had his disappeared attendant-slash-companion who may or may not be named Martin Levy. He was the guy with the tattoo on one arm. Then I had the FBI snooping around and talking about plural investigations. I had Director Tompkins who seemed to have something going on the side. Then I had an ice-blue Audi with a very tenuous link, at least in my mind, to the Federal Building in Minneapolis and to the building where something called the Elite Corporation was housed. Way out there in Edina. And I had a diskette. Which appeared to contain a database detailing years of financial transactions. I wondered where and in what form the money might have been stashed. But since I didn't have access to banking records, I put that question on the back burner. Then I had some fool trying to ice me with a high-powered rifle, no less. I called Catherine and left her a message at both the apartment and her office to say I'd be out all day and I'd touch base later. Then I sallied forth.

★ ★ ★ ★ ★

There were just two messages on my answering machine in the office. One was from my old friend and former employer, Duke Fararra. It had been a year since I'd last talked with the man, and I was almost surprised he was still around. He'd seemed old when I left his employ, and I guess I assumed he'd have retired to Sun City or some other geriatric desert. His message was short and to the point. "Call me," it said.

The other message was more worrisome. It was from my burglaries target, Director Tompkins. He wanted to meet with me as soon as it was convenient. He sounded uptight. I returned Duke's call. As it happened, he was in.

"Duke Fararra. I am surprised to learn you reached out to me."

He hacked gently in my ear. "Excuse, please. Yes, Sean. It has been a while."

"So, how have you been? I sort of thought you'd be retired."

"No, my boy, not just yet."

"So, how may I be of help?"

"I'm not sure. I understand you are involved in the recent demise of a certain Augustus Molinaro. That you are looking in to his death from some kind of bomb."

"I am indeed." I wasn't surprised he knew about my current case. The local P.I. community isn't large, and there are gossips everywhere. But still, I wondered why he was even interested. I mean, I worked for the man a few lifetimes ago, but we weren't exactly pals.

"I was asked to give you a reference yesterday. A woman called who purported to be representing the director of some sort of retirement home. She called me to ask about your bona fides."

"She wanted a reference."

"That is correct."

"Odd."

"Why is that?"

"The Molinaro thing involves a retirement home."

"Yes, of course, Sheltering Limbs."

"It seems coincidentally odd that you'd get a call about me just at this time from someone in that business."

"Not entirely, my boy," Duke coughed again. There was a pause while we each listened to the other breathing. I broke first.

"Not entirely?"

I could hear the smile in his voice. "Not entirely. I'm on the record as the investigator of choice for several chains of retirement homes in this part of the world. If they want to check out the background of an applicant they go to their professional journals, or to their files."

"And what do they find?"

"Ah, dear boy, they find my agency listed with a few positive recommendations."

"Really. And do these places pay you a retainer?"

Duke hacked again and said, "One does. Most do not, but being listed is a great advantage. Such sensitive work, you know. Choosing an investigator from the Yellow Pages, really isn't very wise."

"Yeah. Thanks, Duke." I was surprised he'd given me a reference. I never thought he'd cared all that much. Nice of the old codger.

We disconnected and I mused about the new information.

Chapter 26

Nobody had seen Martin Levy since the bomb killed Don Molinaro. I had a lead or two, but so far nothing had come of them. Maybe I should tail the two bozos who were paying my fee to look into this mess. But there was no telling when they might show up again. I figured I could sit on the Elite address until somebody drove out in that ice-blue Audi sedan, but there might be more than one of those around, even being driven by members of the Elite corps, whatever that was. The telephone rang.

"Hey," said my main squeeze. "I caught you in the office. Things a little slow?"

"Not really, but I occasionally have to keep up with the business side. Right now I'm dusting the file drawers." Catherine sometimes chided me on what were, to her, my sloppy business practices. I heard voices raised in the background. "What's going on?"

Catherine sighed. "I'm at school."

She meant her own school of massage therapy in northern Minneapolis. "So, what's up?" I said again.

"Sean, I hate to do this. I don't like asking you for favors, but maybe you can help this student."

"Hey, babe. You know I'm always ready to help out if I can."

"Okay." Her voice became brisk. Executive like. She'd made a decision. "One of my students has a problem, and I think you can help. Will you at least talk to her? Soon? It's kind of pressing."

"Sure. Is she there? I can come out right now."

"Great. I'll tell Francine and have her wait here."

I leaped in the car and tooled on out to the Minneapolis School of Massage Therapy. In the lobby the receptionist directed me to the conference room down the hall from Catherine's office. Halfway there, the lady herself appeared in the door. I touched her arm, and we went in together.

There was only one other person in the room. She was seated at the narrow table with her back to the windows. She looked up at us. Her eyes fixed on Catherine after a quick flicker of a glance at me. Nervous, I thought.

Catherine smiled and said, "Francine, this is my very good friend, Sean. He's the private detective I told you about. If you'll tell him your story, I'm sure he can help you."

"Francine," I said and nodded. Catherine sat down at the end of the table, and I sat across from Francine. She rubbed her fingers together, and it came to me she didn't want to be there. "Maybe it's hard for you, talking to a stranger," I said quietly. "But let me assure you of a couple of things. Whatever you tell me will remain among the three of us. I'm not going to judge you, no matter what. After I hear you out I may be able to offer some immediate help. Or suggest something. Okay?"

Francine nodded and sighed. I wondered what kind of trouble this young woman had gotten into. Drugs? Booze? Pregnant? None of those seemed like problems Catherine would ask me to help with. Maybe Francine needed a go-between, an intermediary. Had she killed someone?

"I feel stupid," she said abruptly. "Angry, freaked, I don't sleep well any more."

"And she's not concentrating in class the way she started," interjected Catherine. "Which is how we came to this meeting."

Francine blew out her breath, disturbing the blond hair hanging on her forehead. "Here's the deal. I'm a student, a senior at St. Thomas University. In Saint Paul?"

I nodded. I knew where the school was. Way across two cities. A long drive.

"I live off campus in a house with two roommates. Women. Just so that's clear." She waved her shapely hands when she talked. "This all started a couple of weeks ago. We're being harassed."

"Ah," I said.

"Yeah. It started with phone calls. Hangups. Breathing. You know. Then he started leaving paper sacks of shit on the porch. Rachel and Bonnie and I rent this house."

I pulled out a pad of paper and a pen. Sometimes I make notes.

"Anyway, now we're getting burgled. At least twice."

I raised my eyebrows. "You called the police?"

"Sure. They're understanding, and all and they said they'd tell the squads to drive by more frequently, but it hasn't helped."

"You called the cops after the first break-in."

"Yeah. See but then he came in again after that."

"And what did the cops say that time?"

"Not a lot."

"What did he steal?"

"Nothing. He left stuff. He messed around. You know?"

"Tell me."

Francine pushed her hands through her hair and offered up a tentative half smile. Blew out her breath. "It makes me crazy. He pawed through drawers in our bedrooms. Left some of those escort ads from City Pages on the bed. He lay down in Rachel's bed. Under the covers. Sick." She was talking faster and faster. Catherine laid a gentle hand on her arm, and Francine stopped in mid-word, looked down, took a huge breath and slowly blew it out. "Rachel is talking about moving out, at least until the cops do something about this guy, but I can't afford to cover her part of the rent and word will get around so it'll be hard to find somebody else. Even if I wanted to. Every penny is going into my schooling, and I don't want to drop out of massage school."

I nodded sympathetically. "Between Saint Thomas and massage school, you've got a pretty heavy load. Add the amount of time driving from Saint Paul to here and back, I don't know how you manage."

"Motivation," said Catherine. "Harassment aside, I don't want to lose one of my best students."

Something in my makeup reacted strongly to situations like the one Francine described. It came from the same place that sometimes got me into confrontations I probably ought to stay out of. Like whenever I encountered some bozo verbally abusing a woman, I often jumped in without considering whether the woman involved could handle the situation. What Francine was describing really got my juices going. "Do you know how he got in?" I asked.

"Not for sure. I mean I can't prove it, but we think he forced a window on the back porch. There's an easy reach, and it's dark. I mean we've gone around and made sure the screens are secure and the windows don't open very far, but you know somebody could get in if they really wanted to. What am I gonna do?"

"What about the basement windows?"

She looked blank for a moment. Then she nodded. "God. We didn't think of that."

"What do the cops tell you?"

Francine shrugged. "We've told them who we think it is. There's this guy—this creep on campus who just hangs around. Rachel told the campus cops about him but they don't do anything either. The school says he's not registered and he's never approached any of us in public. Everybody says they need proof."

"Okay," I said. "I have some ideas. It'll take me a few hours to get some gear together. Do any of you three have a camera?"

"Rachel has a cheap one. I don't, and I don't think Bonnie has one, either."

I made a note and told Francine I thought I could help her and her roommates out in pretty short order. We made arrangements to meet at their duplex right after supper that evening. Francine left, and I cancelled my standing date with Catherine and boogied on home. On the way I stopped at a Walgreen's and picked up three cheap disposable 35mm cameras with built-in flashes and film.

At home I surveyed my surveillance equipment. I own several cameras, some cheapies some quite expensive, along with assorted control boxes and electronic flash units. I packed a bunch of stuff and at the appointed time arrived at the slightly seedy duplex in the tangle town area of Saint Paul.

The place looked like your typical off-campus student housing. It was maybe one step above the rooming house, but that was it. There were shade trees in front, and the lawn was brown and patchy because it hadn't had any real care all spring and summer. A slender dark-haired, dark-eyed young woman answered the door. She stared at me, waiting for me to identify myself.

I nodded and smiled. "I see you have the safety chain on. That's good. I'm Sean. I assume Francine has told you I was coming?"

The woman closed the door in my face and I heard the chain rattle as she unhooked it. When she reopened the door she glanced down and said, "Yeah, she told us about you always wearing red Keds. But she didn't mention you're so short."

Chapter 27

"You must be Rachel," I said evenly. Even inadvertent cracks about my height didn't faze me.

Rachel looked at me quizzically and then stepped back, gesturing me into the large front hallway. "Yeah, how'd you know?"

"You don't look Scandinavian and Rachel is not a common Scandinavian name. Your dark hair doesn't look dyed. If you press me I'd guess Middle Eastern heritage."

She raised an eyebrow, nodded and turned away gesturing me to follow. "My mother was born in Egypt. What else?" She was obviously enjoying this. She led me toward a bigger room that must have been the living room, judging by the furniture.

"Between nineteen and twenty-two, five-four and right around a hundred pounds."

"Close," she responded.

I walked after her, noting the drapes hanging over a big front window and the shade pulled down over the window on the south side of the house. Next to it, slightly askew on the wall, was a large abstract painting still in its stretcher.

Rachel turned and looked at me, a small smile raising the corners of her generous mouth. "You're pretty good. Oh, of course. You've already talked to Francine. For a minute I forgot. She must have given you a complete rundown. Well, you're right. I'm Rachel." She stuck out her hand and we shook.

"I'm glad you had the chain on the door."

"Well, I'm pretty freaked over this. It's going to affect my grades if it goes on much longer. Besides, we shouldn't have to live with this intimidation. I've been considering getting a gun of some kind."

I frowned. "Not a good idea. Either of the others having similar thoughts?"

Rachel shook her head and raised her voice. "Guys. Our P.I. is here."

A voice I recognized as Francine's answered from what must have been the kitchen. Another lighter voice sounded from down the hall toward the back of the place. In a few minutes the other two women appeared. Bonnie was the youngest of the three, she told me, being a freshman at Macalester College.

"I didn't know frosh could stay off-campus their first year." Bonnie just looked at me and shrugged. All three agreed they were more than a little upset by the stalker.

"All right," I said after we settled in the living room. "What have you done to secure the place?"

"The cops came by after the first time we called. One of them looked over the whole house, and we're doing all the things he suggested," said Bonnie.

Francine nodded. "We've had the windows secured on the first floor here. We paid to replace some of the screens too."

"The landlord said he'd pay us back but so far . . ." Rachel shrugged.

"After the fixes, has he been back?"

The three women glanced at each other. "We aren't sure," Francine murmured. "If he has he's been a whole lot more careful."

"I'm sure he has," said Rachel. "I just can't prove it."

"And you think he's stalking you on campus." I got a chorus of nods and yeses. But none of them could give me more than a vague description of the guy. Tall, sandy hair cut short, carries a backpack, no glasses. Only like a few thousand guys on any campus.

"How did you three get together? I mean, two of you at Saint Thomas and Bonnie at Mac?"

"Bulletin board notices," said Francine. "I met Rachel in class last year and when we decided to room together we found this place and I stuck up notices at Mac."

"And I turned up," finished Bonnie.

They gave me a walking tour of the house. From inside it was pretty secure. The back door was vulnerable and I knew I could pick the two locks in a minute or less. I didn't mention that. Any further upgrading was going to run into serious money, except for nailing the basement windows shut. I doubted the landlord would pop for anything more than that, and I knew the women didn't have the kind of money it would take to upgrade their security even more. Besides, it wasn't their house. What I had to do was get rid of this stalker and restore peace and calm to the neighborhood.

Back in the living room I said, "I have planned a two-dimension program here. First, I want each of you to start carrying these cameras. I fished the point and shoot flash cameras out of my bag. If the guy you suspect of stalking you shows up when you are away from the house, I want pictures of him."

Francine nodded, frowning. "I get the idea, but isn't that a little dangerous? We've given you a description."

"A picture or two could be very important, and it'll be easier if we try to photograph him before he knows we're coming after him. You're not to confront the guy or even try to get closer once you see him. Anything will do, even a back shot. When you're walking across campus or in the parking lot or waiting for a bus, if you see this guy, you grab a snapshot. Don't even look at him. Maybe you'll see him a long way away. Don't go toward him. Shoot the building behind him with him in the frame. Even take a few snaps when he isn't around at all. I want people to start seeing you with cameras as natural. Get the idea?"

All three nodded, Francine a little dubiously, but they took the cameras, examining them and looking through the viewfinders until I was satisfied they had the basics down. Rachel even pointed hers at me and snapped a picture. What I didn't tell them was that each camera was set to record the date and time of each exposure. When their pictures came back I would know if they were all talking about the same person, or might be overreacting a little. It wasn't usual for a night intruder to also stalk a target during the day, and I wanted to verify their sightings. I also wanted to be damn sure I covered the three women as carefully as possible. Since I couldn't accompany each of them all day, and none of us could afford additional operatives required for that kind of protection, I hoped to get this done with minimal hassle and help restore their peace of mind.

"Now we come to the other part of this protection. I'm assuming you are right and this clown is still getting in the house at night. These intrusions have all been at night, right?"

Rachel nodded. "Yes. Well, we aren't sure. It's possible he's been in here during the days when we're all out."

"That's right," Bonnie said.

"Right, I forgot," said Francine. "Once I was gone overnight and another time Rachel wasn't here. It looked like he might have been in the house then." She shuddered.

I diverted with a different question. "Do you want to prosecute this guy?" There was a long pause while we looked at each other. The specter of a trial and the publicity sat on the table in front of us.

"Well, he hasn't done anything really bad," said Bonnie. "I'll go along with whatever you all decide, but I just want him gone."

Francine said, "He's already disrupted our lives. I'd like to see him prosecuted but . . ." Her voice trailed off. Then she said softly, "I'll agree to anything you want."

I asked another question. "This creep doesn't come into your rooms and touch you, right?"

The three looked at me then at each other.

"What?" I said.

Bonnie sighed and said, "I never wear anything at night and my bed covers are usually on the floor by morning. I'm really restless and I hate having to wear pajamas. They wake me up at night. I assume he probably watched me sleeping nude. I've been wearing pajamas, but that's the other reason I'm losing sleep. My grades are gonna suffer if I can't stay awake in class."

I nodded. "Okay. Let's take a look at the house from outside."

They'd gone to considerable expense for three college students. The back door off the kitchen led to a small stoop. The outside light had been rewired and now had a motion sensor so it came on in the dark if anyone came up the steps. They'd trimmed back the bushes around the foundation and pinned the downstairs windows so they only opened a couple of inches. I checked the basement and found a window that was badly rotted so that locking it wouldn't be much protection, and they called the landlord. Meantime I nailed a piece of plywood over it, and we piled some old pails and metal heating pipes over the window so they'd fall loudly if anyone came through there.

After the tour we settled in the living room again. "Here's what I'd like to do if you all agree. I'll set up flash cameras to cover what I think are the easiest places for someone to get in. I can rig a motion sensor to trigger the cameras if someone tries it, but I had to order a new sensor, and it won't be here for a couple of days."

"So what?" asked Francine, "can't you be here until then?"

"You mean in the house?" said Rachel.

"Yeah. Could you sleep on the sofa for a couple of nights?"

We all looked at each other. I thought about my pad. The cats had plenty of food. They wouldn't be happy with day-old water, but they'd survive. I kept a sleeping bag in the car for emergencies like this so there was no problem there.

"Okay," I said, "I can do that." I looked at each of them in turn. After another moment's hesitation, the girls shrugged okay.

I dragged in my gear from the car and set up tripods and cameras, one on the front window, one in the kitchen focused on the back door, and the other on the basement door. Then I moved the car away from the house.

By midnight, things were set, and the women went to bed. "Remember," I said, "I'm on the couch in here. I don't want one of you forgetting and coming at me with a big frying pan."

I'd moved my car a block away after dark to avoid revealing my presence in the house, unless our stalker was paying very close attention. I pushed the lumpy sofa cushions around until they gave me some semblance of comfort and dozed off.

At three in the dark a.m. by my watch, a creaking noise awoke me. I assumed it was a creaking noise because that's what I heard as soon as I became fully conscious. Old houses creak. I knew that. Even my house in Roseville creaks and pops, and it isn't that old. But sometimes my instincts send me a message that the creaking is not normal. This wasn't normal. Somebody or something was on the main floor. Creeping around, trying to be quiet.

I slowly raised up. I hoped whoever it was hadn't heard the change in the rhythm of my breathing and knew I was now alert. I glanced around the living room. There were lots of unfamiliar shadowy shapes, but nothing seemed to be moving. When I could see over the back of the sofa, I peered at the arch that led to the dining room and kitchen. There was definitely something amiss there. The darker presence moved then. No creak. I closed my eyes, ducked down and fired the camera. There was a pop from the flash, a high-pitched squeal and the sound of bare feet running frantically up the stairs.

It was immediately obvious what had happened. One of the women in the house had crept downstairs to the kitchen. Maybe it was a test. Maybe she forgot I was there. I dunno. Maybe she just got a late attack of the munchies. I knew no intruder was going to skulk around the place in bare feet so it had to have been one of the inhabitants.

I smirked to myself and slid back inside my sleeping bag. There were no incidents the rest of the night. In the morning the four of us had breakfast together. I expected one of them to mention the incident. The squeal and pounding up the stairs, even if the feet in question were bare, must have awakened at least one of them, but there was nothing. I didn't even intercept any odd or guilty looks. I decided not to raise the question, and none of the women mentioned the late-night uproar. No one had breached the windows or doors, I was certain of that, but if they weren't talking, neither was I. It didn't matter. I'd have a photograph later.

I arranged to meet Bonnie back at the house late in the afternoon. They didn't offer me a key, and I didn't want to ask for one.

Chapter 28

Even though my car was parked a couple of long blocks away, I approached it with caution, glanced at the gravel I'd scattered around it on the street. Nothing seemed out of the ordinary, but I still held my breath when I unlocked the vehicle and turned on the ignition.

As I drove off I considered whether I was bringing danger to my three new clients. It was always possible, but I was alert and I'd been careful to lose any possible tails. Besides, I didn't think the bomber was after me. There was the question of the mysterious Audi, but there'd been no attempts on my life since that single rifle shot. Even that might not have been a serious try. It could have just been a warning. Sure.

I drove to North Minneapolis and parked in an alley behind an ordinary soiled concrete block building. The place showed no evidence of windows and the single door in the four-story structure was an oversized steel affair. At the very top, old steel or tin caps on the blocks bled orange rust several courses down in irregular patterns. Black smudges littered the surface of the building and effectively concealed small glass panes set flush with the concrete. The trash in the alley against the walls smelled a little. I pressed a small rectangular plate set on the side of the steel door frame. A small speaker/microphone opened. I heard the empty sound of space when it did.

"Sean, happy warrior for the people," I caroled, even though I knew the eyes on the other side of the door could see me from

The Case of the Deceiving Don

one of several hidden cameras.

A clicking sound reached my ears and the seamless painted steel panel in front of me shifted just a little. I didn't check behind me. There was no need. If there'd been another human within fifty yards, the door would not have unlocked. I grabbed the handle and pulled. The barrier swung open easily with no noise on a well-maintained balance system. Inside the overhead light revealed that I now stood in a wood frame cage covered with heavy hardware cloth. When the outside door swung closed and locked, the sliding frame in the cage opened and I went to the freight elevator directly ahead.

I had only to step inside and pull down the gate. The elevator shuddered once and then rose silently to the second floor. When I entered the loft I was on a polished wooden floor. Rows of widely spaced support columns marched in orderly fashion across the entire place. There were no interior walls, but large sound baffles had been installed on the ceiling to reduce sound echoes. The occupant had built a long bench against the entire north wall. It held a variety of monitors, scopes, tape machines of astonishing variety, CD and DVD machines, and test equipment. A single shelf, piled with small instruments and tools hung above it. The smell of smoking hot solder mixed with ozone laced the air and a barely discernable hissing from compressed air that kept the gates of the five film projectors clean tickled my ears. Fluorescent shop lights hung over the scene.

"Chester Patek, master of electronics, at your service," came a quiet voice. I glanced around and saw him stumping slowly across the room, his one full-size crutch under his arm. He was coming from the direction of the single bathroom, half a city block away at the other end of the building. In his hand he held a black box with a short antenna. His remote door and elevator control, I assumed. But what did I know? His teeth gleamed under the short thick blond mustache. Patek looked about the same as the last time I'd seen him. He was a Desert Storm vet, but he didn't seem to be aging at the same rate as the rest of them. I knew he'd lost one leg just below the knee in that action and that he was most definitely a high grade computer genius, along with several other talents he was rumored to possess.

"How's the family?"

"Dandy. Perry is doing great at Breck, and he's starting a folk-rock group. Elizabeth loves Stanford. Elaine's design business is growing. All things considered, we're doing just fine."

You couldn't have said it was so from the flat, inflectionless tone of Chester's voice, or the calm expression on his face. Patek had never, in my presence, exhibited any real emotion. Combat in the desert can do that to you. "A folk-rock band?"

Patek glanced at my feet. "How's your supply of red Keds holding up?"

I shrugged. "Fine. I hear they may be renewing the manufacture of them." So much for personal or small talk. I glanced behind Chester toward a monstrous television screen standing in one corner. "New toys?"

I saw Patek's teeth briefly in what might have been a tiny smile. "Yep, latest thing, High D, plasma, surround sound, DAT, Dolby, satellite reception, plus a few tricks of my own design. I've even upgraded my security system." He pointed back at his blinking, rotating, whirring lair.

I looked where he indicated at a bank of six small color monitors, each showing a different view of the outside perimeter of the building. I knew Patek owned the building and was its only tenant. He'd started his journey to electronic wizardry in high school and honed his knowledge and skills in the Army where he'd lost his foot and part of the leg. His clients were few and paid well. Exactly who they were was not something I was privy to, but I was confident they paid large bucks for his services. I

The Case of the Deceiving Don

was an occasional client only because he seemed to like me and because I'd done a small job for his brother. Naturally, there were rumors among the few who knew Chester Patek and that this building even existed. But there seemed to be an unspoken agreement that outsiders didn't talk about Chester or his family, even among ourselves. Exactly what Patek did, and how he did it, or for whom he did it, was hidden under the calm unruffled surface of his phlegmatic personality and an abundance of caution. He volunteered nothing about his clients or his professional life. For all I knew he could be an NWA monitoring station. Or a mobster.

"I'm sure you didn't answer my summons because you want an update on the family," Patek said. He waved away my protest and continued, "I've made a clean copy of the disk for you, and I finished running any number of tests on the thing. Some of the coded information gave it up to a couple of standard algorithms. The rest is a home-made unique code. The owner of this file assigned a letter and number combination to each of his—or her—clients. Presumably, given the number of combinations I see, he—or she—has committed the code to paper. Even with a supercomputer, it's not likely I could decode that part in a month of Sundays. The code is too complicated to be trusted to memory unless the owner has a prodigious intellect.

"Because the dates and the considerable amounts of money are in plain language it looks to me like whoever originated the disk started out to build an elaborate system and then got tired of it, so only part of it is encoded. That suggests the owner is not a cryptologist or a professional in the code business. Those kind of individuals are usually obsessive about their work. They wouldn't leave this kind of unfinished job.

"Here's a copy of the disk and a printout." He handed me a brown envelope. There was no printing or any other distinguishing marks on it and I was willing to bet a small sum I wouldn't be able to lift anybody's fingerprints from it, other than my own. Patek continued, "I have tried to be sure that my entry into this disk is undetectable. You better know that even your theft of the disk may have triggered a marker of some kind. Assuming you lifted it, of course. But I don't see any indications to suggest anything that sophisticated."

As usual Patek had no way of knowing the disk came from the desk of the director of Sheltering Limbs, and he showed not a trace of curiosity about how I'd acquired it. I hadn't told him I'd already looked at the disk. He didn't need to know. I realized that if Director Tompkins was that computer-savvy, he'd be able to detect that someone had looked at his little record.

"I also wiped any prints."

"Thank you, my friend," I said. We shook hands and I turned back to the elevator. Entering the box, I glanced back at Chester. He was already sitting down with his back to me, intent on his machines and whatever he was working on, dismissing our brief contact as he had with me and most others all of his life. I wondered, as the elevator descended, if Chester Patek was ever euphoric with happiness, or sometimes sad, or mostly somewhere in between. Was there true passion in his life? I wondered if he had even slight mood swings. He never seemed much different in the scattered times we'd had direct contact. I'd met his wife. She was a pretty, intelligent woman with a nice smile, and I also wondered briefly, during my descent, what their life together was like. Just another mystery in Minneapolis.

Chapter 29

My office telephone answering machine offered up no new messages. I did a little business, sent out a bill, cleaned up a report and got it ready for mailing. Meanwhile my brain was sifting through the information I had on Tompkins and his lucrative scam. That scam it was, I had no doubt. Generally speaking, directors of nursing or retirement homes really didn't require secret files of off-the-books income and payments to unknown parties. I still couldn't connect those payments to the death of Don Molinaro. The puzzle was too fragmented to suggest a decent picture.

It got along to afternoon and no sexy, willing, voluptuous, woman had graced my office, nor had anyone come through the door, waving gun or subpoena. Fact is, nobody at all came through my door, so I took myself off to Saint Paul and my newest crop of clients. They being Francine, Bonnie and Rachel, the three college students who were apparently being harassed and stalked.

When I got to the house, I found Bonnie waiting alone.

"Hey," I said when she opened the door on the chain as I had cautioned them. "How was your day?"

She unlatched and ushered me to the living room where my sleeping bag lay stuffed behind a chair. Bonnie watched me check the cameras to be sure our unwanted visitor hadn't triggered them while the house was empty.

"Here's my camera," she said. "I only saw him once today,

and he was a long way off. I'm afraid these won't be much use in identifying him."

"Don't worry about it," I responded. "I expect we'll have a lot of useless pictures. All we need is a couple of good ones. Keep the camera until you use up the twelve shots."

Bonnie sat down on the couch while I checked the wiring and the triggers on the living room camera. There was something on her mind. I could detect that.

"Mr. Sean," she finally said. "I have a small confession." She paused and then the words tumbled out. "That was me last night, in the kitchen?"

"Okay," I said. "No big deal. Did you just forget?"

"Not exactly. Sometimes when I'm stressed out I walk in my sleep. I think that's what happened. But you see, I don't always remember it and usually I just walk around a little and go back to bed. But it's embarrassing."

"I don't know much about the condition," I said sitting down across from her, "but I'm pretty sure shocking a sleepwalker awake isn't a good idea."

"The thing is," she nodded, "I almost always sleep in the nude, so the picture . . ." her voice trailed off. "I wouldn't want it to show up on the Internet some day."

I smiled and nodded back. "I get it. Well, you shouldn't worry. I don't have a web site, and I'm not gonna give or even show the picture to anyone else. When the film's developed, I'll give you the negative and the print right away. But we have to figure out something to prevent this happening again. Any ideas?"

The door opened and her housemates trooped in.

Bonnie lowered her voice, saying, "I have some medicine which usually helps. Basically it's a sleeping pill. It works almost all the time. But apparently not last night."

Rachel and Francine, still chattering between themselves, scrabbled in pockets or purses to find their cameras. They each had taken a couple of snaps of the man they said was stalking them.

"Okay," I responded. "I bet as soon as we nab this guy your stress level will go down a lot."

"What's up?" asked Rachel, coming into the living room.

Bonnie just shrugged and changed the subject with a slight shake of her head. I wondered if either of her friends was aware of Bonnie's affliction as it appeared she didn't want to talk about it in front of them. It occurred to me that some of the stalking Francine and Rachel had told me about might have been Bonnie on one of her nocturnal sojourns around the house. I wondered why she didn't wear pajamas of some sort, to deflect her embarrassment. But what did I know about the mental state of apparently intelligent college women?

The next afternoon I was back. Francine had called to say they'd used up their films. I took the cameras to a darkroom run by a guy I trust. When you're a P.I. with a limited budget it helps to have a bunch of various resources to call on.

Paul ran the films from the cameras through his machine and gave me the prints thirty minutes later. I took them back to my office and coded each according to who had taken them. Since they were date and time stamped already, it was pretty easy to correlate them. Sure enough, as I had half suspected, the guy they were suspicious of showed up on the same day at almost the same time on both campuses. Macalester and Saint Thomas aren't that far apart, but it would have been impossible, given the time stamp. What's more, although the target of their pictures looked a little alike, it was obvious it wasn't the same guy when you put the pictures side by side.

But one of the men the trio had targeted did appear in several shots on two of the three rolls. Both Francine and Rachel had pictures of the same guy in various locations on the campus.

They hadn't captured any evidence of unusual attention, and there were a number of joint classes which all of them could have been attending. Coincidence piled on coincidence. After eliminating the useless and shots of the mistaken clone, I found that one guy appeared in eighteen of the thirty-six pictures. There were a couple of other shots which were possibles, but the subject was too far away to be sure. In one great shot, Rachel had captured the guy in a small group looking right toward the camera from only about twenty feet away.

I bundled up the pictures and went back to Saint Paul. All three of my clients were home studying. I laid out the pictures I had selected and explained why I thought they were sometimes seeing their stalker when he wasn't actually there. The pictures were far more persuasive than my words alone would have been. Having accomplished that goal, we set out to identify the one guy who could be the stalker. We agreed that this medium-height, sandy-haired, chunky guy who appeared to be a student, was most likely our midnight intruder. "Great. Now all we have to do is identify him."

"What about your camera shot from last night?" Rachel asked.

"Still in the camera," I said, not looking at Bonnie. "I'll get that taken care of tomorrow." I was pretty sure we hadn't had an intruder, but in deference to Bonnie, I wasn't going to mention that.

"A poster," said Rachel, abruptly. "We'll take this good shot and make up a poster that says STALKER! DO YOU KNOW THIS CREEP? Then we'll make a bunch of copies and plaster them all over campus."

Sounded good, but Bonnie raised an objection. "This isn't proof. What if we're wrong? We could ruin this guy's life."

"Yeah," said Rachel. "That's the idea."

"Let's find out for sure before we accuse him. But we can make copies and ask around, get an ID."

I chimed in. "Exactly. Find out who he is first. Then I can watch him and catch him red-handed, so to speak. It'll probably be quicker than trying to get the college administration to identify him."

Rachel agreed to take the best picture to Kinko's and get some copies made. I promised to get back after dark. I borrowed their telephone and called Sheltering Limbs. After a short delay, I heard Blanche grumble, "What? Whosis?"

"Blanche, it's me, I'm coming out there to see the director if he's in and—"

"Oh, he's in all right. I can see him from where I'm sitting.' Which is what I do most of the time, you know."

"Good. I'll call him. Now here's what I'd like you to do . . ."

Chapter 30

Twenty minutes later I walked into the retirement home and smiled at the receptionist. "I'm Sean," I proclaimed loudly. "I have an appointment with the director." I glanced along the hallway. Blanche Essen's gray-haired head peeked out from a doorway about halfway along. I recalled that it was the door to the day room and was almost opposite the director's office.

"Of course," the receptionist nodded. "He's expecting you."

I sauntered down the hall, studiously avoided looking at Blanche. Director Tompkins' office door was ajar. I rapped and pushed it open. Tompkins was on the phone, and he nodded and waved me in. By the time I'd grabbed a chair at the side of his desk, he'd concluded his call and hung up.

"Thanks for coming over. I wanted to follow up on our conversation about Mr. Molinaro."

I wondered if Tompkins had some direction from his principals. I wondered who his principals might be. I also wondered what family he might be associated with. Or was this a joint effort? I wasn't really up on the mob's current configurations. Didn't know how much they still operated or how much power they still had. Ever since Gotti had been sent off to federal prison, things had been pretty quiet, far as I knew.

"Mr. . . . Sean. I've had a call from a member of Mr. Molinaro's family. I take it you have been making inquiries?"

First time I'd heard the Don had any surviving family. Interesting. Nearly all my inquiries had been with officialdom,

The Case of the Deceiving Don

except for my two clients. Were they family? "It's as I explained. Because Augustus was blown up in front of my house, I've taken a certain personal interest."

"Apparently, your, ah, personal interest has disturbed some members of Mr. Molinaro's family. They are devastated, as you might imagine over his abrupt demise and . . ."

Raised voices from the hallway caused Tompkins to stop talking for a moment and glance toward his office door. I hadn't closed it all the way when I'd entered. "The family has released me at least partially from my obligation of privacy, and they would prefer I handle any further questions you might have."

"Might I have the names of these family members?"

Tompkins smiled faintly and declined to name them, again citing their desire for privacy. I wondered if the family was paying Director Tompkins to deflect me from the hunt for final answers. I also wondered what kind of family we were referring to. "That would certainly be convenient," I smiled back, thinking that since apparently no one had been to visit Greasy Gus for several years, Tompkins probably had more immediate information than the family, blood relations or not.

"Is there anything you can tell me about Mr. Molinaro's situation prior to his coming here?" I went on. "Prior to his stepping behind the veil of secrecy."

Tompkins frowned. Raised voices from the hallway intruded again. I heard someone, probably a nurse, remonstrating with someone. It sounded like she mentioned Blanche.

"I'm not sure—" There was a sudden crescendo of voices and a loud crash from right outside Tompkins's office. "Excuse me!" he blurted, and leaped out of his chair. As he disappeared into the hall, I slid smoothly to my feet, nipped around and yanked open the bottom left drawer of his desk. In my other hand I held the envelope containing the disk I'd stolen earlier. With the cleanest of movements I slid the envelope into the last section of the drawer, closed said drawer and trotted across the office, almost in the director's wake.

In the hall minor confusion reigned. Tompkins and two attendants bent over a figure on the floor. Blanche Essen was half lying against one wall next to her overturned wheelchair. Close beside her was an old man in—no surprise—a second wheelchair. Blanche was hurling verbal imprecations up at the man.

"I've told you before, George, don't be coming around that door so damn fast! You think you've always got the right of way?"

"Listen, you hot-rodder!" I could see George was trying not to laugh. "I had inside position! You cut me off. Again! Are you okay?"

"I guess so." Blanche's imprecations aimed at George faded into unclear mumbles, but she shot me a single hot glance and I nodded, gave her a surreptitious quick thumbs up.

"I think," said Tompkins with a grimace, straightening. "These two ought to be checked by the doctor."

Neither wheelchair had sustained more than a few scratches, so staff got Blanche back in her chair and wheeled both combatants down the hall as they continued trading verbal taunts. Tompkins and I returned to his office.

He shook his head. "I'm sorry about the interruption. I hope this doesn't give you a negative impression of our establishment. Things like this almost never happen." He glanced down and frowned. Then he bent, and I figured he was securely closing the bottom drawer which I might have left slightly ajar.

"I would like to better understand Don Molinaro's position. Before he came here. He retired to Sheltering Limbs? Correct?"

"Quite right. He lived in Pennsylvania. He had a very successful construction business, I understand. He was a widower, and his sons are deceased."

Rubbed out by rival mobsters? I wondered. What I asked

was, "Exactly where in Pennsylvania did he live?"

"Harrisburg. Actually a suburb called Mechanicsburg. After his wife died, he decided to leave the area and chose to come here. I wasn't directly involved in those negotiations. I believe I mentioned to you earlier that I came here right after he did."

"Minnesota seems an odd choice. Why didn't he move to one of those Southwestern enclaves, like some of his business associates?"

Tompkins looked baffled. "I'm sure I have no idea."

"Was this mysterious Martin Levy who danced attendance to Don Molinaro with him when he first came to visit Sheltering Limbs?"

Tompkins shook his head. "Again, I wasn't here, so I can't say positively, but it's my understanding from the records," he gestured minimally in the general direction of the row of file cabinets, "that he did arrive with Mr. Molinaro." Tompkins pulled back his coat sleeve and glanced at his watch. "I have an important appointment downtown. I'm sorry to cut this short, but you can certainly see me again if there is anything else you wish to know."

" 'Sall right. I'm running a little behind myself." I stood and we shook hands like business buds do. Right. He'd not told me anything I didn't know, but he had confirmed some suspicions. It was pretty clear to me at least that someone somewhere was yanking his chain. I stopped at the front desk and asked the woman there, "Do you know if there is anyone still on the staff who was here fifteen years ago?"

She thought and then said, "I guess I don't know. Some of the older long-time residents might remember if there is."

I waved it off. "That's okay it was just an idle question." It wasn't, but I was pretty sure Blanche could find out for me. I wanted to pin down the relationship between Levy and the Don if at all possible. If I could do that I might have that elusive thread that would unravel this whole thing when I gave it a good yank. On the other hand, I mused to self, suppose Mr. Martin Levy turns out to be a plant, say from one of those obscure federal agencies with acronyms whose meanings are likewise obscure. Now that would tell me something else about the situation, and I wouldn't need to chase the bugger. Then the problem would be finding out who and why the Fed was staying so close to a retired Don. Difficult. I couldn't exactly appeal to the Freedom of Information Act, could I? I softly whistled a tuneless melody and went out into the blazing sun.

Chapter 31

Rachel was hyped.

She grinned hugely when she opened the door to my rap, bouncing on her toes, which imparted an interesting jiggle to her apparently bra-less chest. She led me to the living room. I heard rattling in the kitchen. Bonnie poked her head out and said. "Hi. We're celebrating."

I raised my eyebrows in a questioning manner—it's something I practice. Non-verbal communication is often more effective than mouthing words.

"Yup," Rachel said, slamming herself into the corner of the couch. It shuddered. "We identified the creep."

"The stalker?"

"Yup," she said again. "I made some copies of the picture, and we all asked around today. Several people recognized him."

Bonnie came in and handed me a cold beer. She had one for herself and gave the third to Rachel. "Francine's in class at that massage school."

"And?" I said.

"And his name is Kirkus Andronikos."

"No shi—kidding," I said.

"Kirk Andronikos," gushed Rachel. "I looked it up on the Internet. His first name means church and the other is, like, victory of a man, or something like that. There's a Roman spelling too."

"Yeah," I said. "Shakespeare used Titus Andronicus in one of his plays." Both women looked at me with mild amazement.

I smiled. "What, you think just because I'm a detective I don't got no education?"

They laughed.

"Look, it's good that you've identified him, but this isn't over. I don't think we should confront him until we've got real proof. I'd like to catch him in the act, so to speak."

"Exactly," the women chorused.

"That means you have to be here with the cameras some more nights, right?" Bonnie said. She tilted her head and swallowed some beer.

Rachel leaned over and grabbed Bonnie's free hand. "Hey," she said softly. "It'll be okay. We've been looking for a chance to tell you we know."

"You know?"

Rachel nodded. "About your sleepwalking? We've known for quite a while, but it was obvious you didn't want to talk about it. So we didn't say anything. And it didn't happen very often anyway."

Bonnie was starting to get a little teary. "Oh."

"One night you tried to walk out the front door."

"What did you do?"

Rachel smiled. "Francine just took you by the shoulders and slowly turned you around. I was in kind of a dither. But she shushed me and changed your direction and after a minute you went back upstairs to bed."

Bonnie sniffed and wiped her eyes with the back of her hand.

"Have you been sleepwalking all your life?" I asked.

"Maybe. I guess so. I don't really know. Nobody at home talked about it if I did. I'm afraid my family will think I'm crazy. I had an aunt once. She was in some kind of place, an institution? I heard my mother say she walked in her sleep.

That's why I never talked about it here when I figured out I was doing it."

"Stress," Rachel said. "I looked it up on the Internet. You're stressed out over this creep and school and stuff. I bet if we nail this Kirkus guy, things will be better."

"How do you know you're sleepwalking?" I asked. "I thought people who did this usually didn't know unless they woke up in strange places."

Bonnie nodded. "The meds keep it under control mostly. What happened the other night? With you? Same thing happened a couple of months ago." She looked at Rachel. "Remember Tim?" Rachel and Francine traded glances.

"I dated him for a while," Bonnie went on. "He fell asleep one night on the couch after we'd been studying. I went to bed, but then I came down later and woke him up."

"You were naked," Rachel said, smothering a smile.

Bonnie looked surprised and nodded. "I know. It's stupid but I just can't stand to wear anything in bed. Gets tangled and keeps me awake. I've tried all sorts of clothes. Anyway, Tim thought I was coming on to him. He grabbed me and kissed me. That woke me up, and I fought him off. Scratched his face." A tear rolled down her cheek.

Rachel took up the story. "The fuss woke me, and I started downstairs. By then they were yelling at each other. Tim took his books and stormed out of the house. I went back to bed, and Bonnie never saw me."

"Ended that romance," said Bonnie. "I kind of liked him too."

"I looked it up on the Internet and called the Sleep Clinic in Minneapolis," Rachel went on. "I said I was doing research for a paper.

"I guess Francine and I can take turns watching you, Bon.

Sleep in the hall or something until this gets settled," Rachel said.

"You guys will have to work on the sleepwalking thing," I said. "Not my area of expertise, but maybe a psychologist could help. Or the local sleep clinic. I'm here until we nab this guy. I thought the motion sensors would be here by now. Your couch is not the most comfortable, but it'll do."

Francine arrived later that evening, and the three women congregated in the kitchen for a while. I dozed off until Francine woke me. It was a few minutes before midnight. "I'm off to the sack. Rach and Bonnie are already upstairs."

I waved, turned over and hauled the sleeping bag over my head, being sure the camera triggers were near my fingers. I woke up at one-thirty. No biggie. I just woke up. There wasn't a sound. I was falling back into the black when I heard a distinctive sound like light sawing. It sounded like when I was cutting screen to size for a new window at home. Somebody was cutting screen. At the back of the house. I peeked over the sofa and realized the back door security light was off. Guy was trying to force entry from the kitchen. Not smart. Climbing through open windows or doors was one thing. Breaking and entering was a higher class offense. I shifted on the couch, and one hip ground into my Chief's Lightweight S&J I was wearing under my clothes. I hadn't told the women I was carrying. Didn't want to cause any additional fright. Debating now.

I could leap up and confront the perp, thereby avoiding more property damage. Or I could wait until he came in range of the camera so I'd have documentary evidence. I waited. The scuffling noises from the back of the house went on. After a minute the sawing noise stopped. I could almost chart the goof's progress, and I clearly heard the sound of his feet hitting the kitchen floor when he came through the window. I hoped the women upstairs weren't hearing anything.

The Case of the Deceiving Don

After a silent ten count I opened my eyes again and glanced just to the right of the kitchen door, opposite my place on the couch. For some reason the eye sees better in dim light if you don't look directly at the subject. Dunno why. A dark figure was barely discernible framed in the doorway. I triggered the two flash units and gave out an inarticulate yell as loud as I could. Sort of an imitation Tarzan. It all produced the desired result.

Intruder froze for an instant like deer do in the headlights, and then bolted back the way he'd come. Only this time he didn't climb carefully through the window. He dove through, banging the frame and hitting a low bush just outside. I heard him grunt when he hit. By the time I reached the window, gat in hand, he was legging' it across the back yard toward the alley.

"Stop, or I shoot!" I yelled. A cliché, but what the Hell.

He didn't stop.

I didn't shoot.

Chapter 32

The cops came and examined things by the glare of their mag lights. Eventually they left after making several suggestions we'd already thought of and promising to be back when it was light.

About seven-thirty I heard someone creeping about the kitchen trying to be quiet. It was Bonnie. I declined the offer of coffee. I nailed the kitchen window shut, then I packed up my stuff and went home to Roseville. By eleven I had the developed and printed film in hand and went off to see them again. I had a major disappointment. Our intruder was wearing a mask that made absolute identification almost impossible. Must have been really hot under that hood.

However, there was enough hair showing to convince me it was our Mr. Andronikos. What's more, he'd left some bits of himself behind. I found a smear of blood with a fragment or two of skin on the window frame. And there was a bit of cloth, apparently from his shirt, snagged on a piece of branch in the damaged bush he'd crashed through.

There was more. The cops had arrived and found footprints in the soft earth beside the basement windows. It looked like he'd tried at least two other ways in. I turned over the pictures to the Saint Paul authorities. I didn't think the guy would be back. Unless he was several bricks shy of a full load. It was clear the cops now took the incidents very seriously, and I figured they'd pick him up in short order.

I headed for the office. I didn't see any Audis that matched my shadow. I had hardly finished scanning the mail that had collected, dumping all but a couple of bills in the wastepaper basket when a well-suited, short-hair knocked politely and eased on in. He had a dark complexion and from across the room his manicure looked clean and neat. His left hand dipped into his breast pocket and he flashed a gold badge at me. It was petite and looked real.

"Rozan, FBI," his mellifluous voice told me.

I stood up and offered to shake. "Sean, P.I." I responded.

A flicker of what might have been a smile went over his face. I gestured to the chair but he declined. "I'm advised you are looking for a man named Martin Levy."

"I may be."

Rozan nodded once. Economical, this dude. "You don't want to find him."

"I don't?"

"You know that saying?"

"Excuse me?"

"If you do, we'll have to kill you?" He smiled at me.

I waited for the rim shot, a cymbal crash, something.

Nothing. First time I could remember hearing a joke from a member of the FBI. Maybe they're trying for a new, friendlier image. Maybe he wasn't joking.

"You want to expand on that?"

Rozan shook his head. Briefly. "No, sir. Mr. Levy is not a criminal, nor is he involved in any direct way with the murder of that recently deceased gentleman, Augustus Molinaro. We suggest you look elsewhere."

"Okay. Are you guys following me? In a late model ice-blue Audi, perhaps?"

"No sir. Other than the subject of Mr. Levy, we have no interest in you or your activities. Good morning, sir."

I almost expected Mr. FBI man to salute or pivot, but he just turned and sailed on out of my office. Message delivered. Odd, to say the least. I sat down to ponder.

Pondering led me, with almost no evidence, to a tentative conclusion. Levy could be one of two things. He might work for the Elite Corporation as private security which had been hired to protect Don Molinaro. There was a good deal of that going around these days. That's the only way that rather obvious tattoo on his arm made sense. The usual government agencies would never hire or keep a man with that kind of body decoration. Then I remembered something Ricardo Simon had told me in passing. His daughter came home one evening with a large and obvious tattoo on one ankle which caused a family uproar until she explained that it was temporary. The dye, she had told her steaming parents, would wear off in a few weeks. And it had. So maybe Levy was using such a decoration while he was a deep undercover agent for our government and was funneling info from the dead Don to a gang task force. Or something like that.

Huh. I was inclined to take the Fed's word for it. Erase Mr. Levy from the equation. Made life a lot simpler. Now I was gonna backtrack Mr. Molinaro with greater concentration. I'd still like to ask Levy a few questions, but that appeared impossible to arrange. Since Levy wasn't my mad bomber, somebody else was. Since the FBI had come to tell me to get off Levy's trail, they felt my hot breath getting too close. Ergo, it was my letter to Elite that caused the reaction. I was cool with that. I like that word. Ergo.

From my casual stance, leaning against a large elm tree at the edge of the Saint Thomas campus, I watched ragged streams of ragged college students going raggedly between the buildings. Most followed the concrete walks, but there were always a few who took shortcuts across the grass. I was hoping to spot my target perp, Kirkus Andronikos. My information said that most afternoons after classes were over, he left campus walking in this direction. Yesterday the information was wrong. Today might be better. Saint Thomas had no student registered as Kirkus Andronikos and the nice motherly woman in the Records Office refused to tell me whether she recognized the picture we had. There was more than one tall sandy-haired student on this campus.

The cops had taken the evidence left by the intruder to the lab for DNA typing but until we had other DNA linked to a known individual, our sample was useless. The cops would, with a little pushing, assign some resources to finding the guy, but that all would take time and I was impatient to nab this bozo as soon as possible. I figured a little intimidation, directly applied, would make the problem go away. I also wanted to get something with his DNA we could match to the sample now on file.

A tall dude carrying a dark blue backpack materialized from a side door and started my way. He was tall enough, just over six feet, and I turned away so it looked as if my attention was somewhere else. When he passed, I let him get a few feet down the way. Then I followed, my white-soled red Keds soundless on the sidewalk. I was taking a small chance. He could bolt, and I wouldn't be able to keep up in a foot race, short as I am, but I thought I could hold him by playing on his curiosity. He might want to know just how much info I had.

"Andronikos," I called.

He hesitated, then swung around and looked at me. I fired off three quick frames from my motor-driven Nikon.

"Do I know you?" he said. He planted his feet on the sidewalk in front of me, shifted his back pack to the other shoulder. "Why the pictures?"

"Maybe I'm a talent scout. Maybe I'm hunting fresh models."

"Yeah, right," he snorted. "Or maybe you're the tooth fairy."

I noted a bandage on his upper arm just where the short sleeve on his shirt rested. "Or maybe I'm hot on the trail of a burglar."

"Not my thing, man." He jigged up and down on his toes. By now I was in arm's reach. I moved a little closer, invading his personal space. He stepped back.

"Or maybe I'm trying to identify a stalker."

"Hey, I don't know what you're talking about. Back off, man."

I whipped an enlargement of the masked creeper out of the envelope I was holding and shoved it at him. He took it and stared at it. His mouth hung open a little. I hoped he'd drool on the photograph. Then he dropped it.

"I don't know nothing," he protested and turned to walk away.

"How'd you hurt your arm?" I called. He gained a couple of yards when I stooped to retrieve the fallen picture. I was careful to handle the picture by the corners when I slipped it back in the envelope. Now I had his finger prints as well as his DNA.

"You stay away from that house, Andronikos, you hear me? And keep your distance from those women. Otherwise it'll go harder for you." He only increased his pace into a lope I couldn't hope to match. I didn't try.

Chapter 33

I took my fingerprint-tainted enlargement across town to the spanking new BCA lab on the East Side of Saint Paul. They already had a case number from the Saint Paul PD. I handed over the envelope with the picture and signed a statement that I'd collected the fingerprints and DNA from a certain individual and the picture had not been out of my possession since the encounter. I also called Parker, the cop handling the college stalker case, to tell him about the print and then hightailed it to Minneapolis and my cozy office.

It was time to get back to a concentrated effort focused on the deceased Don.

Since I now considered Martin Levy a dead end, it made sense to look into Molinaro's other associations since he'd come to Minnesota. And I wasn't going to forget about that slimy toad, Tompkins, either. I called Blanche. Not surprising, she was available and would be glad to see me that very afternoon.

We met in the day room just inside the door where she'd crashed her wheelchair. Blanche was already there when I arrived, her custom vehicle snuggled into a corner facing the door. I sat with my back to the room and handed her a bottle of pricey water. "I don't know why you drink this stuff," I said. "What's the matter with the tap water around here?"

"Nothing, sonny. But the glasses and cups they have don't fit my cup holder. Whereas . . ." she grinned at me and dropped the bottle neatly into the fabric holder hanging on one arm of her wheelchair. It fit as though the holder was designed for the bottle. "So, what's up?"

"Are you okay? I didn't expect a kamikaze attack as a distraction."

"Shah." She knit her plucked eyebrows at me. "Not so loud. We don't wan' anybody to know, do we? I'm fine. Only one little bruise on my leg. You want to see? Anyway, if that fool George hadn't been coming' so fast there wouldn't have been any problem at all. Besides, it all worked out, right?"

I nodded.

"An' you aren't going to tell me why we set up that little distraction, right?"

"Right," I said. "At least, not today. I'm glad you two didn't suffer any permanent damage. Now listen. I've learned a few things, but you have to keep them under your hat, so to speak." I was deliberately appealing to Blanche's sense of conspiracy. Plus, I wasn't sure if there were staff or inmates at the home who were in Tompkins's pocket. "We can forget about Levy. I've learned that he was here on some kind of assignment. He probably works for the government."

"Which department?"

"Blanche, I don't know. I suspect if I found that out, they'd have to kill me."

She cackled out loud. "Okay, sonny, I got it. What else?"

"I'm pretty sure your director is getting some money on the side, but I don't know who from. Yet."

"What for?"

"That I don't know either. Yet. I have to find someone who was staying here more than ten years ago, from before Tompkins came in as director."

"You mean somebody who's still above ground?" Blanche grinned at her own crack.

I nodded.

The Case of the Deceiving Don

"Try Willie Sutton."

"Who?"

"Willard. You know. Johnson. Our janitor. The guy who keeps things running around here."

I nodded. Then I had another thought. "You know who Willie Sutton is—was?"

"Sure, big time bank robber in the thirties and forties. I think my uncle actually knew 'im. One of my uncles. He never said it, you know."

"Never said what?"

"One time he was asked why he robs banks?"

I nodded.

"Sutton is supposed to have said 'because that's where the money is.' My uncle said some reporter made it up." She grinned.

I could see Blanche was gearing up to tell me a story. I didn't want to take the time but then I thought I wasn't that much in a hurry, and I could tell Blanche loved a new pair of ears.

The phone was ringing when I unlocked the door to my office. I nipped across the room and scooped it up before the answering machine cut in.

"Yeah? This is Sean."

"Sean?"

"Yeah, it's me."

"You sound different."

"Than what? And who is this anyway?"

The caller laughed and then said, "It's Parker, in Saint Paul. Since you've been so helpful with this stalker, I thought you'd want to know. The lab confirmed the prints as a match to those we lifted at the women's house. The DNA will clinch it. Andronikos is the guy. And he's in the system. We're picking him up today."

"Thanks for the heads-up. I'll tell the women." I called the house but there was no answer except the answering machine. I left the good news on the recorder and then located Francine in class at Catherine's massage school. I told her the news. The telephone went almost silent for a long time.

"Oh, God, I'm so relieved. I can't thank you enough, Sean." She sounded a little teary. "I'll tell the others right away."

I turned my attention to the report by Chester Patek taken from the tracks on my purloined disk. The more I looked and studied the columns of figures, the more I thought I should just go to the cops with the info. My difficulty lay in the questions that would be asked about how I came by it. Anybody who kept track of the movement of substantial sums of cash was bent. In my world view, that was a given. Maybe the money was funny, and he was some sort of banker, hiding the payments from the tax guys, or maybe Tompkins was being paid for some kind of illegal activities.

My bet was on the illegal service. Or tax avoidance. So I called my tax guy. Actually our tax guy. Catherine turned me on to Michael Meaney. He knew more legal ways to avoid excess taxes than anyone I knew. Plus he kept up on things.

"So, Michael, how are things in the tax biz?"

"Good afternoon, Mr. Sean. What can I do for you today?"

I immediately fell into his extra-formal means of verbal communication. "I have this document which indicates that a certain individual is receiving large regular cash payments, apparently off the books. I'm not entirely sure, but the schedule appears to be partially in code." I went on to describe the contents in some detail.

"Is this an official document? That is, was it issued by an institution? Is there a letterhead?"

"No." I figured I better not tell Meaney the document was printed off a stolen computer disk.

The Case of the Deceiving Don

"Can you link it to this individual's salary, presuming there is one?"

"Yes and no. Yes he has a salary, and no this schedule appears to be completely separate. What's more," I said, "remember it's in some sort of code. The sources of the cash. They're in code."

"Yes, I remember. Does this individual declare the payments you seem to have found as income?"

"I don't know. I don't have access to his bank records. Or his tax reports."

Michael was silent for a few seconds. "It sounds suspicious to me. But why would this record be maintained, especially since it appears suspicious on its face?"

"I don't know, Michael."

"If you knew the disposition of the funds, that would help. It would point to reasons for both the money coming in and going out. It would be particularly helpful if you could identify the person or persons to whom the funds were being dispersed."

"To put that in plain language, if I knew who got cash from this fund and what for, I could get a handle on its legitimacy."

"That would be correct."

"Thanks, Michael."

"Not at all, Sean. Call any time."

"Sheet. Talk about helpless. If I had those answers, I wouldn't need Meaney. Well, since I was the detective, I decided to get to detecting. Detecting sometimes involves speculating. Suppose, I speculated, Director Tompkins was a mob keeper? Suppose he took care of aging Dons or button men or lieutenants who needed to be kept away from inquiring feds?

Chapter 34

I left. As I went to my car I checked my surroundings. That had become automatic. No Audi, nobody carrying a rifle. All rightly then! At home in Roseville I fed the cats and called in a message for Catherine. Then I sat down with a single malt in just a dribble of water and thought about what I knew. What I came up against was what I didn't know. Too much. I figured I could make a case against Tompkins for some kind of illegal money fudging. What I didn't know was the motive for killing the Don. Huge hole. Nothing the cops nor I had dug up gave so much as a glimmer of a reason. And since there didn't seem to be anything in his recent past or the local scene, I was beginning to conclude that the bomb had been planted in retribution for long past events.

That meant Pennsylvania. Mechanicsburg specifically. Even if I went there, being on unfamiliar ground would make any detection very iffy. What's more, I was short on desire to tangle with the mob, even with a historical element. Let dead bodies stay buried was my motto. Unfortunate in my line of work, I guess.

Mildly disgusted, I threw on my sweats and a grotty pair of tennies and went for a walk. My path took me around the rear of the Sheltering Limbs. There I chanced to meet again the nurse I'd encountered by the smoking tree along the path on the day the Don was blown away. "Hi, there," I said. "Remember me?"

"Of course," she said, sucking in another lungful of carcinogens. "You're the dude who's trying to figure out who killed Mr. Molinaro."

"Correct. Anything interesting to tell me since I saw you last week?"

"No." She bent and stuck her butt—her cigarette butt—into the sand in the coffee can at her feet. "But your big buddies have been around again."

"My big buddies?"

"Yeah. The guys you asked me about the other day." The nurse went on to feed back to me my description of Mr. Buzz Cut and Mr. Hands. Now this was more than passing strange. Were these guys checking up on me? Conducting their own independent investigation? I didn't like it.

"They were just here. They are probably still here. They spent a long time with the director."

"But you have no idea why."

"No, but Mr. Tompkins sort of showed them around. You know, he gave them the tour people usually get when they are planning to dump a relative here."

"Ah, I see."

"Except that neither of them seemed all that interested. They didn't look like the kind of people who'd be putting a relative in the home. One of them, the one with the really big hands, he looked totally bored. Like he'd rather be almost anywhere else."

Mr. Hands had never, in my presence, looked anything but bored. I figured that might be the only expression in his repertoire. I wondered if he looked that way when he was having sex. Not for long. The nurse started walking toward the building, giving me the message her break was over and she had to get back to work. She went in an employee back entrance, and I continued up the street and into the parking lot between the building and the county road. Among other parked vehicles, I saw a blue, late model, Audi and a large black Cadillac, both empty. Neither one sent any vibrations to my antennae. I heard the sound of a door opening. Male voices issued forth. One of them sounded like Tompkins. I risked a glance behind me. It wasn't hard. I bent over and retied my shoelaces and peered back through the gap between my leg and my elbow. Sure enough, I was right. There was Buzz Cut and Mr. Hands with Director Tompkins. They parted while I watched. They didn't shake hands. Their body language didn't send friendly messages. On the other hand, they didn't appear adversarial either. I squatted down until I was crouched against a dirty Chevy. You don't want to make sudden movements if you wish to avoid attracting attention. I stayed there for a few minutes while I tried to determine if the two thugs were coming my way. I heard a car door slam, then another. It sounded liked the doors on the Audi. Not that I've made a study of car doors, but the sounds came from the right direction.

A moment later an automobile drove out of the lot. I stood up, hoping Tompkins wasn't standing in the doorway waving a fond farewell. He wasn't, and the blue Audi was leaving the lot, heading west. I continued my walk. I had another piece of the picture. Tompkins, for whatever outward reasons that the nurse had seen, was connected to Mr. Hands and Buzz Cut. My experience told me it was entirely too coincidental that those two would just happen to interview Tompkins and hire me all in the same ten-day period. My two clients must be on a dual mission, both relating to the events at Sheltering Limbs. And the nurse I had encountered a little while earlier had said "again," as in "Your big buddies have been around again." That told me Buzz Cut and Hands had been to see Tompkins at least twice and they had at least once mentioned my name within hearing of that nurse.

I had, on the occasion of one of their visits to my office, made a couple of photos of those two gentlemen. Just in case.

The Case of the Deceiving Don

Maybe now was case. I went home, retrieved the best photo from the file and drove over to the Roseville PD. Helen Lasker smiled when I was escorted to her cubicle.

"Hey, Sean, what's up? I guess you haven't run afoul of any more shooters with your name on their minds."

"Nope, and I'm even starting to relax a little."

"So you have a picture for me?"

"I do. If you have these two in your files, I'd like a little background."

Lasker waved me to a chair and went to her computer. After staring at the screen and frowning while typing for a while, she nodded and glanced over at me. "Got 'em both. They're in the system. Not ours, which is still deficient in some respects, but in the national database. I'm printing mug shots for you. The guy with the oversized hands is one Myron Cole. His friend is Dennis Hamilton. They aren't mobbed up although the question keeps getting asked. Some mob guys appear to be known associates of these two. Both have done time for age assault and robbery, that's with a weapon. I can't imagine what they're doing out here in our fair city."

"Where are they from?"

"Last known address is in Mechanicsburg."

"Mechanicsburg?"

"Yeah, that's in—"

"Yeah, I know. Pennsylvania."

Chapter 35

"It's looking more and more like I have to fly out to Pennsylvania to crack this thing." I was lying on the sofa in Catherine's living room. My head was in her lap, and she was playing her agile trained masseuse's fingers over my forehead. It was very pleasant.

"Seems like a long trip for a client you don't have." She left off smoothing my brow and sipped her rum and tonic. Then she put her cool fingers back on my head. I shifted one shoeless foot to the top of the back of the sofa. We were having a relaxing evening alone together after one of her outstanding salad-focused dinners. Low-carb, high-protein diets notwithstanding, she continued to eat all things in moderation. Me too, especially when in her most excellent company.

"I know it does. But I'm getting nowhere at this end. My two suspicious clients, Buzz Cut and Mr. Hands aren't leading me anywhere and Tompkins, while definitely involved in some way I have yet to fathom, is, for the moment anyway, a dead end."

"My, what a long, complicated sentence. Wait a minute."

"What?"

"Look," Catherine said. She shifted slightly under me and grabbed the remote control for the television, which was muttering away in one corner of the room.

I rolled my head toward the set and squinted at it. When the sound came up to an audible level the announcer was saying,

". . . office building on Central is home to a variety of businesses."

"Hey," I said, "that looks like my building."

"Witnesses told our reporter on the scene that a loud gunshot and breaking glass first alerted them to something out of the ordinary. The night maintenance man for the building owner said he heard running footsteps immediately after the gunshot but saw no one."

I sat up and leaned toward the television. The camera was focused on a street scene dominated by what was definitely my building. There was a crowd just standing around weirdly illuminated in the flashing lights of two squad cars at the curb. When the camera tilted up to the third floor I realized with a jolt we were now looking at the window of my office. The broken window of my office with one of my new blinds hanging askew.

"Oh, Sean. What's happened?" Catherine stood and reached for me.

I squeezed my arms around her in a brief hug and then stepped away, heading for the door. "I'll call you as soon as I find out."

I grabbed my keys and slid feet into a pair of red Keds by the door. I didn't bother to tie the laces until I was in the elevator and dropping to the parking garage under the building.

Fifteen minutes later I parked in the lot in my usual spot behind the building and let myself in through the rear door. By now it was dark enough so I was unable to tell if there was an ice-blue Audi around. So far, I hadn't seen any cops, but when I got to the third floor a uniform was standing in the hall. He was positioned so he could keep an eye on the elevators and the broad length of the hall itself. When the elevator door slid open and I exited, the cop swiveled his head and stabbed me with a steady look.

I had my wallet in hand and open. "I'm Sean, I think

something happened in my office."

"You got that right." He checked my ID and waved me on. "See the detective." He pointed.

I trotted to the door to my office, dodging around another uniform who was fixing to put up some of that yellow plastic Crime Scene tape they use. I looked in at a scene of complete chaos. Jesus. My office was a wreck.

The desk leaned against one wall up on end. The drawers had been pulled and their contents tossed about. My poor inoffensive and elderly bent-wood hat rack lay on its side. It looked like one of the horns was broken. The file cabinet was on its top in the corner and the three drawers were elsewhere. One apparently had been thrown against the wall. It was empty, bent and it apparently had been slammed down the wall, making a long gouge in the plaster. I could see my belongings were scattered helter-skelter around the room. It looked like whoever had searched the place had vented serious anger on the furnishings. The computer lay on its side and the monitor, its torn cords dangling, lay across the room, screen smashed. My blood pressure started to rise, and my heart hammered with anger.

But that was as nothing. The attention of nearly all the authority in the room and then mine focused on the crumpled body lying below one window.

The man in charge, a detective I didn't recognize, turned around and looked at me. "You are?"

I identified myself again and then behind us I heard the elevator door open. Hard heels came rapidly down the hall. The detective glanced over my shoulder and shifted slightly to block the door. "Detective Simon," he said. "Something I can do for you? We have everything under control here."

Ricardo Simon laid a hand on my shoulder and said, "No problem, Ed. I came when I heard the address. This man is a friend of mine. Are you okay, Sean?"

The Case of the Deceiving Don

I saw the detective in front of me relax infinitesimally. He'd caught the call and didn't welcome intrusion from another detective.

"Yeah," I said. "That's not me over there by the window, and I wasn't here when this happened. But thanks for coming," I murmured. Then I looked again at Ed, the detective in charge. I swallowed once and said, "Can I go in?"

Detective Ed nodded. "Yeah. Take a look at the DB and see if you can identify him. But keep your hands in your pockets."

"You'll find my prints all over the place." I did as he asked and stuffed my fingers in the front pockets of my khakis. I walked slowly across the office to the body, avoiding what had become trash littering the floor. When I leaned down I realized that I knew the man—sort of. His medium brown brush-cut hair was recognizable even though his face was mashed into the corner beneath the window where the wall and floor met. His legs lay akimbo on the floor and his left arm hung on the frame of the smashed window, holding up his shoulder. I surmised he'd been standing at the window when he was murdered.

A crime scene tech knelt at Buzz Cut's feet. "You know this man?" said the voice of the detective from above me.

I nodded. "Yeah, sort of. He was a client."

"What's his name?"

"Dennis Hamilton. He's a felon and he's in the system." The tech did something I couldn't see with his gloved fingers. Then I made a conscious decision. Since I never wanted to play around with the mob anyway, and since this guy and his friend, Hands, had never honestly identified themselves, I felt no obligation to claim client privacy. Maybe that was against the Private Eye Bible, but right then I didn't care. I had already figured out what must have been going down. "Let me explain."

I told the detective about my relationship with the two felons I'd named Buzz Cut and Hands, and he made notes. I suggested he call Helen Lasker at the Roseville PD to get more about the investigation into Gus Molinaro's death. He made a note of that as well. I also knew he'd get a pretty good report on me, but I didn't see any reason to mention that.

"So you know this guy, not well, just enough to identify him. What do you think he was doing in your office?"

"I have no idea. But looking at the condition of the place, I'd say he and his friend were searching for something. Information, probably. I think someone said after the shot he heard running footsteps. That was probably his colleague, Myron Cole, the guy I dubbed Hands."

"You didn't let him in?"

"No, detective, I didn't. No, and it wasn't me running away."

I glanced at Rick Simon and then said to the other man, "Look, I have a strong hunch this was accidental, that the shooter thought it was me at the window." I went on to explain the earlier shooting incident. The detective made more notes.

"So you didn't let him in, have a falling out, and then whack him?"

It wasn't a seriously intended question, but I didn't like his tone. Simon, who knows me too well, saw the warning sign, shuffled his feet and leaned toward me. "No," I said, "I didn't whack him. I was home with my friend Catherine when we saw the news report. I came right down, late as it is."

"Okay, we'll check it all out, Mr. Sean. I'm afraid you can't use your office for a while. You can go, but stay available. We'll want you to check for missing items in the morning." He turned away, dismissing me. I started to head out with Rick when the detective gave it one more shot.

"Nice tennis shoes, by the way."

Chapter 36

Downstairs, Rick Simon touched me on the shoulder and said, "Look on the bright side. At least for a while you can rest easier. Whoever shot that man thinks he got you. You're safe for the time being."

"That'll last about a day." We were standing together on Central in front of my building watching the occasional car go by. At this hour there was still traffic, and the bars had just closed for the night. A gang-banger in a low-rider with tuned mufflers and heavy-duty bass speakers cranked way up cruised by. The sound was so high I could almost see the car shimmy. I wondered how long the occupant's hearing would hold out under the assault.

Ricardo and I split and went our separate ways. I walked toward the lot where I'd left my car, around the corner just outside the perimeter of official vehicles crowded beside the building, feeling easier than I had for days. I was looking back toward the front of the building. It's something one shouldn't do on the sidewalk because I crashed full stride into another person. Fortunately she wasn't walking very fast in the other direction.

I hit her with my leading shoulder and using my usual lightning reflexes, grabbed her before I knocked her flat on the concrete.

"Oaf!" she said.

"Oh, sorry," I said. I had her by the arms, and we did a little two step in a circle to bleed off some of the energy and regain our balance. "I should be more careful. I hope I didn't hurt you."

"No, no," she said, twisting out of my hands. "I'm all right." The woman slid away and went on, angling between two patrol cars without a backward glance. Apparently she was planning to jaywalk across the street. I went around the corner to the parking lot and my car. The back of my neck itched suddenly. I had the feeling I sometimes get that I was being watched. I spun around, but there wasn't anybody there. Naturally not. I got in the car and drove back to Catherine's apartment. Ninety minutes later I sat bolt upright, wide awake in the dark bed. "Wait a minute!" I cleverly exclaimed.

"What?" murmured the lady beside me.

I slid up toward the head of the bed. "I just realized something. I've seen her once before."

"What? Who?" Catherine quickly falls deeply asleep and when she wakes takes more than a minute to return to the aware world. She rolled closer and kissed my hip.

"The blond woman I almost decked? I mentioned her, didn't I? When I was leaving the office. I thought when I walked into her she wasn't a complete stranger, and now I'm sure. A week or so ago, I bumped into her on Central looking at the building register." I concentrated on the woman's image, trying to build a stronger mental picture. It became harder to do. Catherine's fingers ventured over my bare thigh.

"In fact," I said, "I'm pretty sure I saw her before that, even. But where?" I slid out of bed and padded to the little table in one corner of the bedroom Catherine uses for an office. I sometimes dropped my diary there. The one I often carry to note expenses, for observations when I'm on surveillance, like weather and odd facts that help me recall specific circumstances. Helps me when I have to testify or submit expense claims, or write client reports.

I paged back, but I didn't find any reference to encountering a blond woman under notable circumstances. I made a note of it in that day's page and while I was writing I remembered the first time I thought I'd seen her. On the beach. I couldn't swear to it, but now I was 90% certain that same woman had been at Lake Johanna the day after the bombing of the Don. A dark-haired woman in a modest two-piece suit, I thought. And later that same day I'd encountered a woman, a blond, in the lobby of my building. And now a blond on the street after a shooting in my office.

I was all but certain all three women were the same person. I had no real evidence of that, but sometimes I leap to judgments. Sometimes I'm wrong. Other times I'm right. Either way, this definitely bore looking into. More questions. I made a quick note and went back to my sleeping beauty.

Morning came entirely too soon. Catherine had no pressing appointments or needs so we had a leisurely breakfast and enjoyed the sun streaming through the dining room windows.

After I told her about the three apparent sightings, she said, "So you seem to have a stalker."

"Maybe. I tend to think there may be a more sinister aspect to this. It's just too odd that this woman shows up at the beach where I swim occasionally, then twice more at my office building."

"Particularly on the same night when somebody gets shot in your office." We both were silent for a moment. Some of the bright light of the day seemed to have disappeared. Catherine leaned over and squeezed my arm. We'd talked about this a few times. She didn't like the sometimes violent aspects of my career. And she worried about what my cases might be doing to my personality, my attitude toward life, as it were. I'd told her more than once that if she ever found me changing, she should kick and scream and make sure I knew it too. Of course, kicking and screaming were not in the lady's tool kit, but her management skills were extensive.

Catherine Mckerney had inherited a substantial stock portfolio from her father and had built a small massage business into a school and some big-time contracts with local businesses and public institutions. Her passage through the business world was marked by success and admiration. Catherine could project a tough-as-nails persona when the situation called for it. I knew she'd use it on me if it ever became necessary.

As it was, we talked a little about the dead guy. I wondered aloud if he'd had a family, if they would ever be found and whether there were children. It was sad. "I guess he was a bad dude, and I won't lose any sleep over his demise, but it looks like whoever shot him was gunning for me. I've got to figure out who that is and if that woman I keep stumbling over is involved."

"Why don't you ask her, the next time you see her?"

"Take a direct approach."

"Might save time and worry. Maybe it really is coincidental. Or benign."

"Hah! You don't believe that for a New York minute. And neither do I." I picked up the phone and called the cop shop. I wanted to get back into my office, assess the damage, and get about replacing or repairing what was needed.

The news was not good. The cops wanted at least another 24 hours. I went to the Sheltering Limbs to talk to Blanche.

"So, sonny, what's going on in the outside world?" Blanche was staring out the window from her wheelchair when I finally tracked her down in the game room, or social room, or whatever they called it.

"I came to ask you the same thing."

Blanche scratched her gray head. "Mr. Tompkins ain't here.

He left rather abruptly 'bout an hour ago. Looked a wee bit upset, he did."

I wondered if he'd heard about Buzz Cut's violent demise. Maybe he was on the run.

Chapter 37

The call had come at two that morning, but I wasn't in my office to receive it. No surprise there. After talking with Blanche, I took myself to the library. In these days of Internet research we sometimes forget that large publicly supported repository of considerable knowledge and information. So I went to the library. Under the heading of Mafia in the electronic catalog I found several references to Allenwood and the families of Pennsylvania. After a couple of hours of reading I thought I was on the right track. Federal authorities believed there was a well-developed clandestine system for funneling information and other stuff in and out of the various prisons in the area.

There were several references to my main man, Don Augustus Molinaro. Nothing definitive of course, but when I put it all together it appeared likely, to me at least, that Molinaro had been blown away because he knew too much about something that had happened in the past. But what? And how was I going to deduce what it was?

When I returned home from the library there was a message from Catherine inviting me to join her for an intimate supper that evening. I accepted with alacrity. Then I turned to the other calls. There were only three, of which two were telemarketers of one stripe or another. But the third was intriguing.

"Sean. We need to talk. Meet me south end of the Stone Arch Bridge tonight, three a.m."

The Case of the Deceiving Don

Sheet, I thought. How bad a cliché is that? While I wasn't sure who it was, the voice was definitely familiar, and since the call had come in at two a.m., I assumed the caller expected me there that very night. Or the next morning. I didn't think he meant an hour after the call he'd placed. I'd definitely missed that one. Meeting him that night interfered with at least some of my plans for the evening, but I was used to juggling my obligations.

It was a typical mid-summer night in Minnesota. Hot, moist, thick. It was nigh onto three in the morning and the pavers under my tires chuckled and popped. That's what they're called, pavers. Basically, they're a kind of brick, and they replaced mud and gravel on a lot of Twin Cities streets in an earlier century. Some places they called 'em cobble stones. Later they were dug up or just coved over with asphalt. In this historic district of the original village of Saint Anthony, hard by Saint Anthony Falls on the Mississippi River, in spite of their unevenness, the pavers had been exposed and many re-laid to add a bit of nostalgic ambience to the neighborhood. With the later bar closing installed by the legislature and various city councils, there were still a lot of people about here in the dead of night and numerous cars parked at the curbs. In an earlier time, three in the morning would have been pretty dead. Maybe my mysterious caller was hoping for the anonymity of a crowd.

I was driving slowly south, more or less along the east bank. That put the river on my right. My caller had said to meet him at the south end of the famous Stone Arch Bridge. The bridge actually connects the east and west banks of the river, but because of the orientation of bridge and river at that particular place, the east end of the bridge was actually a little south of the west end. People sometimes get confused about that. Makes clandestine rendezvous problematic—or something. A patrol car went by in the other direction. I felt the cop's eyes on me for a minute, registering, assessing my presence. Not for the first time I wondered why I was indulging my caller. I might learn something significant, but more than likely, I wouldn't. I was a little more relaxed than I might have been because the site was open. It would have been difficult to sneak up on me, or even to get a shot off. The lighting and the closed up building on this side of the river all worked in my favor.

He was wearing a western-style straw hat and dark narrow-legged pants. But no high-heeled boots. His shoes appeared to be dark cross-trainers. The hat was pulled low on his forehead so his face was shadowed from the ugly orange overhead light that fell on us. He was white. His dark blue or black short-sleeved shirt revealed skinny arms and knobby elbows. I judged he was around forty, maybe a little older, and around 160 pounds. He appeared reasonably fit. He was leaning against the railing on the bridge looking sort of down toward the water and when I got close enough he said "Mr. Sean." Quiet voice. Flat, no discernable inflection or accent. Not nervous. Like the voice on my machine.

"That's me," I said. I didn't ask his name. I figured it was a waste of breath. He didn't ask me for ID, either. I was pretty sure anything that transpired here wasn't going to end up in a courtroom under oath.

A nocturnal bicyclist rode slowly by, tires faintly hissing on the pavers. I leaned on the same railing facing the man about four feet away. My instincts told me he wouldn't take it kindly if I moved closer. He turned his head and seemed to look past me. I had the feeling he was checking for observers. I'd already done that. I was feeling just a mite exposed. After two murder attempts I was jumpier than usual.

"You came alone."

The Case of the Deceiving Don

"Yes. Your call indicated this was to be a private meeting."

"You wired?"

"No. That stuff is expensive, not always reliable, and I can't recall the last time I had a need for it."

"Who killed Dennis?"

"Dennis?" For a moment I was taken aback, as it were. I recovered quickly. "Oh. Dennis, the man I called Buzz Cut. I don't know."

"Wasn't you."

"No. I was home watching TV. I think he was searching my office and somebody made a mistake. Whoever did it saw a shadow on the window blind, thought it was me, and pulled the trigger."

"You get shot at often?"

"No, but it happened not too long ago. In my office that time as well. Missed me then, too." I made an effort to keep my voice laconic. I didn't want this guy to think I'd been freaked. Or that I was a little freaked at the murder of Buzz Cut in my office.

"So you're satisfied whoever shot Dennis thought he was aiming at you."

"That is correct."

"And it's not related to the Molinaro thing."

"I don't believe it is. I haven't come across anything that would lead me to think there's a connection. I could be wrong about that."

My inquisitor shifted away slightly to take more weight on his off leg. I can't stand hip-shot like that for more than a few seconds. I guess the stance pinches a nerve in my back, or something.

"You worried about being offed?"

The tone of his voice changed. I'd had a feeling right from the beginning that the guy was graveling his voice and trying to use language in a different manner from his normal voice. All by way of concealing his identity. "Do you want to get to your point? It's late, and I've got a full plate tomorrow." I didn't, but he didn't have to know that.

"Have you discovered anything about Gus Molinaro's background?"

"Some. He came from Mechanicsburg. That's in Pennsylvania. Just a short ride south of Allenwood, the federal prison."

Straw Hat nodded once. "Do you know where Martin Levy is?"

"No," I said truthfully, "I don't."

"We think he was planted on Gus."

I remained silent. None of my business what this guy and his companions, or family, thought. The less involved I could stay, the more likely I was to come out of this without any excess baggage. I rolled to my left and placed both elbows on the rail. Stared down at the water. It put me a little closer to my companion. I had my face turned toward him and could see a figure on a bicycle coming toward us along the bridge. Under the orange lights he was wearing a helmet, loose ankle-baring pants and a baggy tee shirt. He kept both hands on the handlebars and pedaled at a steady pace right on by us. Didn't so much as glance our way.

"I think you've got a tail," I said. "Unless that cyclist is one of your minders."

Straw Hat tensed slightly. "All right," he said. "Somebody will call you." He stepped toward me with his right hand outstretched. Almost automatically I responded, and we touched palms in a quick handshake. The folded piece of paper had some glue on it so it stuck to my palm and I curled one finger around it. I turned slowly and watched Straw Hat walk steadily across the street and disappear in the dark at the end of the bridge. I never saw him again.

Chapter 38

"Why don't you just drop the whole thing? Sean, you don't have a client anymore."

"I took money from Buzz Cut and Hands—Myron—to find out who killed the Don. Even if technically I was already studying the case before they showed up."

Catherine sighed. "Could you pay it back? Stubbornness will get you hurt. And I sure don't like your entanglement with some crime family."

We were having lunch at Emily's Deli on the north side of Minneapolis. "Funny you should mention that. After the other night when Dennis got killed in place of me, I thought about it. If I could find Myron. Get a message to whoever is pulling his strings. But my sense is he's probably still legging it all the way back to Philadelphia, or wherever he was when they sent him here to back Dennis. I figure he's gone from our life."

"So you think he's the one with the muscle and the other one was the head honcho. Did you find out anything more about that prison? The one in Pennsylvania?"

I nodded, my mouth full of cabbage leaf roll. Swallowed. "As a matter of fact, my inquiries are starting to pay off. It seems Don Augustus Molinaro was indeed something of an important fellow in that area. He reportedly had a lot of contacts, not only around town and among law enforcement folks, but in the prison system as well."

Catherine cocked her head and frowned. On her it looked

good. "You mean among the federal employees of the prison?"

"Sure. Is that so hard to believe? Remember this was years ago when the FBI was mostly looking into things that set off J. Edgar's paranoia. Apparently they didn't vet some of the prison employees as carefully as they should. Plus, for anybody willing to run a few risks, there's still a lot of money floating around.

"Anyway, the passage of information from wise guys inside the walls back and forth to other wise guys outside must have been a tidy business for someone with the right contacts. Probably still is. Don Molinaro was apparently one such guy. His network was fairly extensive. I'm also informed by the usual unnamed sources that he even contrived to have a guy sent inside the prison for a couple of years because his network had gotten thin."

"So what does all this have to do with bombing poor Gus?"

We finished lunch and went to the car. "I'm still not entirely sure, but I have an idea the root of this bombing lies in Molinaro's information network and the other tasks he did for the guys."

In the car, Catherine leaned close. The garlic on her breath made my eyes water. "So what's next?"

"I take you back to school where you indulge in a little mouthwash, and I go to Roseville and talk to my inside contact."

"Blanche," she said, popping some minty gum into her mouth.

When I got to Sheltering Limbs, they informed me that Blanche was in her room. After a short delay, I was directed to the second floor and along to the southwest corner of the building. When I knocked and was bid enter, I found Blanche in a sunny room with several vases of fresh flowers on the dresser and a small table at the foot of her bed. Her window looked out on the hilly grassland between the building and the playground a couple of hundred yards distant.

"Howdy, sonny," she greeted me from her bed. It was apparent that she'd been in bed all day and had enlisted some help in a little combing and primping before I was allowed into her presence.

I leaned over and bussed her on one cheek. "How are you doing, my friend?"

"For an eighty-year-old who's lived a hard life, and whose plumbing doesn't always work right, pretty good. What's your story?"

She sounded weak and a little discouraged. "Never mind my story. Look at all these flowers. I guess I have some competition." I dragged a chair closer to the side of the bed. Blanche manipulated a control on the side away from me and the bed frame made a grinding noise while it lifted her into a more upright position. She turned her head and looked out the window while I waited.

"Saw a fox runnin' out there the other day."

"No kidding," I said.

"Sure, sonny, sure. Now what can I do for you?"

"Tompkins still among the missing?"

"Yep."

"I'm interested in the rest of the staff."

"There's a lot of turnover in these places. Who wants to spend their lives taking care of cranky old codgers like us? Fact is, though, this place has less turnover than lots of 'em. So, you now thinkin' the Don was sent on his last journey by one of the nurses?"

I nodded, "A possibility."

"Smells better'n most, too." She grinned, forgetting or no longer caring that she wasn't wearing her dental fixture.

I fished out my little notebook. "You told me that there were three people still here on the staff who came before Tompkins.

Anybody who came right around the same time who's still here?"

Blanche squinted at me. Then she smiled. "Y'know, I never got to go play blackjack in Las Vegas."

"Excuse me?"

"I sure hope the Twins make it to the playoffs this year."

I started to think she'd lost it completely. Then she raised a hand to cover her mouth but I could tell she was about to bust out laughing.

"All right, serious, bud. Yes, there are two people I can think of right off who have been here at least five years. Besides that nice young man who cleans up the place."

I assumed she was referring to Willard Johnson. I'd already talked to him and he was easily in his late fifties, but I suppose it's all in how you look at life—and how long you've been looking at life.

"Most of the regular staff has only been here a few years, in fact we got a new night nurse just last week. Nurse Betty came about five years after Mr. Tompkins did."

"Ahh," I said. I made a note. "Which one is Nurse Betty?"

"Hmmpf," she said. "Medium height, pleasant enough, maybe a little serious. A little overweight. She has short brown hair."

"Any distinguishing marks? A tattoo, maybe?"

"She smokes. Chews gum and uses some sort of disgusting mouthwash to cover it up, but I know she smokes."

"Thanks, Blanche, you're very helpful, as always." I leaned in and pressed her hand where it lay on the white sheet. Her wrinkled skin seemed even thinner than the first time I'd met Blanche and I thought I could see the slow pulse of her heart in the veins on the back of her hand.

Her thin lips turned up a little and I saw that her eyes had fallen nearly shut. Blanche was drifting off. Rustling movement behind me caused a turning of my head. A tall angular nurse I didn't recognize came into the room. She went to the other side of the bed and reached her fingers to Blanche's wrist.

"Do you know Nurse Betty?" I asked.

The woman looked blank for a moment. "No, I don't think so. Oh, did Blanche give you that name? She has a nickname for everybody here, just about. She calls me Heron, Nurse Heron. I can't imagine why."

I smiled and thanked her and left Blanche's room.

Chapter 39

So, who was Nurse Betty? Since I wasn't privy to Blanche's system for bestowing nicknames, and the nurse apparently didn't have a visible tattoo, identifying her was going to be a problem. On the other hand, there were only six RNs spread over all shifts who worked in that place. I went for a walk around Langton Lake. And what was with the guy on the bridge? Who needed late-night clandestine meetings with mysterious strangers? I sure didn't. Especially ones in which the exchange of information was minimal at best. The piece of paper he'd slipped me had a telephone number and a few words. The words, in black from a gel pen, said I should call only in a dire emergency. The area code was somewhere around DC. Who cared? If this was some kind of Mafia service number—killers rented by the day or week—or maybe a leg-breaker by the hour, I didn't need it or want it.

What I wanted was to talk with Nurse Betty. Walking back toward home after circling the lake I saw a female figure standing by the side of the path, a few yards from the back of the retirement home. Oh yeah, the smoking tree. I'd seen people here before. Staff from Sheltering Limbs came out here, even in poor weather to stand by the tree during their smoking break. There was a tin can on the ground where they stashed their butts. No litter that way. I'd noticed that the label on the can changed whenever the can filled up, so at least they were neat about it. The woman swung around and looked at me. She took one more puff then swiftly bent and stubbed out the end of her cigarette. A long plume of smoke erupted from her pursed lips and disappeared on the summer breeze over our heads. I recognized her but I didn't know her name.

"You're that detective," she said.

"That's me," I smiled.

She dug in her pocket and popped a piece of gum into her mouth. "Filthy habit, but I just can't quit. At least, not yet."

"Do you know Blanche?"

"Sure, old lady in two fifteen. One of the Wheelies. Always around. I sometimes see her late at night wandering the halls."

We started walking slowly toward the back of the building. "She assigns names to the staff, I understand. Do you know someone she calls Nurse Betty? Another smoker."

The woman frowned. "No, sorry, I don't think so. You'll have to ask around." She fluttered her fingers in a good-bye wave and disappeared into a back entrance. The odor of her habit went with her. I went home. I stopped at the mail box and sure enough, the mail had arrived. As usual it was a big pile, consisting mostly of ads, a few bills, and one larger than normal brown envelope.

A strange feeling came over me. I'm not one to ignore strange feelings. I didn't think twice. I took two quick steps to my right, away from the mailboxes and glanced swiftly all around. Nothing suspicious. No silver or ice-blue late model Audi in view. Only two curb-parked cars at all. No people. Everybody on my block was either at work or staying indoors in air-conditioned comfort.

The sun shone, a bird or two twittered. Nothing out of the ordinary. So why was the back of my neck itching? No revelation came to me, so I took the stack of mail and loped across the hot street and up to my front door. Inside I sat and tore open the brown envelope. It was what I had expected, copies of stories I couldn't get off the Internet. I'd hired a public relations firm in Philadelphia to run down additional information for me on smuggling at Allenwood. This was their report.

Folded once was a stack of six sheets of paper. They were printouts or copies of news reports, mostly several years old. One was from a TV network Internet site; the others from Eastern newspapers. Each one reported on information-passing shenanigans at the Federal Prison in Allenwood. Each told how a network in the prison, moving information back and forth over the walls, had been operating for a number of years. Many years. Confirmed my information. These stories didn't mention that Don Molinaro had been the Don in charge of the illicit information network, but that didn't matter.

Each also reported that information wasn't the only thing that was passed. The list in one story was extensive and varied. Drugs, presumably concealed in various bodily orifices. Apparently some mules were caught, but the authorities admitted there were drugs in circulation at the prison. Other things were smuggled, including guns, knives, lock picks, semen, photographs, baseballs, handballs, swatches of clothing, a wrist watch, keepsakes of various kinds. In and out, the illegal, clandestine, traffic went. I set the story aside and read the rest of the material and the rest of the mail as well.

After a few minutes I looked at the list again and stopped.

Semen.

What?

Pretty bizarre, I thought. But then I considered the subject some more. Were macho gangsters in prison trying to impregnate wives or girlfriends? Why not? And if, for a substantial fee, you were a Don in a position to assure clients that sperm-loaded semen passed over the wall would be delivered in a timely manner to the person of choice, you might have a lucrative side bar to the information and drug-smuggling business. I thought about it some more. Read some more.

One intrepid reporter had talked to several prisoners. One guy, in for life, was quoted as explaining that he wasn't ever getting out and his wife wanted a child, his child. So he managed to impregnate her. He wouldn't say how he got his sperm to his wife, since conjugal visits were not allowed, but he assured the reporter that indeed the deed had been accomplished. With the article there was a small picture of a clearly pregnant woman. She was identified as the wife of the inmate who'd been interviewed. Authorities were quoted elsewhere in the piece saying they were considering charges.

How very fascinating, I mused. But how did this connect to the death of the Don in question?

The more I thought about it, the more possibilities arrived. I discarded several as being so ludicrous that no one would try them, much less believe them. Suppose the Don was paid a handsome sum to accomplish the transference of seed and failed the mission? He wouldn't want to repay the fee, if there was a way to avoid it. What might an unscrupulous person do in that circumstance?

The answer was immediately obvious. Substitute seed. How would Ivan Inmate know? How would the recipient know? Suppose, twenty years ago, when Don Molinaro was running this smuggling and information service, he contracted for a princely sum to see to the impregnation of an important Mafioso's wife. And suppose it didn't work. Maybe the Mafioso had a low or non-existent sperm count. Maybe the first try didn't take. What does the desperate Don do?

Why, he makes a discreet substitution. The woman gets pregnant and years go by. The Don retires to Minnesota. He's out of the mainstream and low in profile. But the Feds keep him under surveillance with the man who's been inside the Don's organization for a while. One Martin Levy, aka who knows, comes west with him to keep him company in his little nest. But then, those twenty years go by and along comes DNA. DNA tests prove that little Johnny or Jilly is not the offspring of VIMafiosoP. That could very well be grounds for murder. That could be motive to send a hit man to Minnesota where the Don was retired.

I explained all this over dinner that night to Catherine. When I finished she looked at me and said, "You left something out."

"What?"

She smiled and took another sip of wine. "C'mon, tiger, how'd they get the man's sperm out of the prison? Inquiring minds want to know."

"I didn't think such subjects ought to pass the delicate ears of proper young ladies such as yourself." That brought a most unladylike snort from my companion.

"All right. The passage of a small amount of seed—"

"Sperm," Catherine amended.

"Sperm," I agreed, "from hand to hand would be as difficult to detect as the passage of these other items. I mean, look at this list."

"And," she prompted.

"Various smuggling techniques were tried. Sperm produced by the inmate was wrapped and inserted in different objects which were then tossed over the wall of an exercise yard, to be picked up by passing confederates."

"Seriously?"

"Would I kid you? That's this reporter's story, and he's stickin' to it. Smuggling sperm was problematic, according to one report, because sperm is fragile and the little critters don't live long outside the body. Coordination was always crucial, and there's one instance in which the timing went awry. A car with a big sunroof passed down the county road outside the prison while a man stood in the opening waving a large net presumably to catch the tennis ball, in this case, which was hit over the wall at a prearranged time. Problem was, when the catcher made a pass. No ball came over the wall. So they turned around on the road, passed again and this time, missed the ball. Gendarmes appeared. When the car was stopped a mile or so away, the occupants insisted they were netting insects in a county project. Apparently, the deputy who stopped them got to laughing so hard he let them go with a warning.

"So what happened to the tennis ball of sperm?" Catherine was now giggling almost constantly. "I'm sorry, Sean. It's tragic, but the images that come to mind—" she waved her hand and turned her face away for a moment, shoulders heaving.

"The tennis ball in question was retrieved by prison authorities and when tested, found to have been injected with sperm. By then, the sperm was dead. It had laid out in the hot weeds that summer day for too long."

It was both sad and comical and while I wasn't sure how I would ever prove the motive, I felt in my gut I had the right one. But I still didn't have a killer.

Chapter 40

The beer I was drinking was cold and hit my spot. How come, I asked self, if, as the nurse I'd just met by the smoking tree had suggested, that staff all knew their own nicknames, she hadn't mentioned hers? That would be normal, self answered. I also recalled seeing that same individual at that same tree twice before, once right after the Don got blown away. Or rather up. Blanche had mentioned, hadn't she, in an off the wall way that one of the nurses smelled bad. Could she have meant the cigarettes? Self then suggested that since the Don was the only one killed by the bomb, it was logical to assume whoever triggered the bomb must have had line of sight to the bomb-ee trying to minimize collateral damage. The death of innocent civilians would not have been a good thing if the deed got traced. I would check my theory.

Finished beer. Brushed teeth. Trotted around the block to Sheltering Limbs. "Excuse me," I said to the sweet lady at the reception desk.

She smiled and nodded hello. We were becoming old friends. "No, I'm sorry," she said to the microphone hanging on the side of her face, "Director Tompkins is out of the building." Pause, frown. "No sir, I'm sorry, I have no idea when he will return."

She removed the headset and wiped the mike with a tissue. "Dear me. He was upset. No call to use such language."

"I'm just going to run upstairs for a minute. I'm sure you

The Case of the Deceiving Don

don't mind," I smiled at her and she gave me a tentative nod. "Meanwhile, can you find the duty roster for last week, the day the Don was killed? I just need to check something. That's much appreciated. Thanks."

I turned away and headed for the stairs. Sweet face receptionist was doing things for me that she should not do. But it was benign. She had seen me so many times, I was sure she thought I had the run of the place. I took the steps two at a time. The white soles of my red Keds only squeaked a little as I trotted to the second floor. Down the hall, I dodged residents, many of whom shuffled or wheeled about minding their own business. I was in luck. Room doors were open so my intrusions were minimal.

I rapped hard on the jamb of the first. "Excuse me," I called to the empty room, "I just need to check your window." From that east-facing window I could see the top of my house but nothing of the street. Whip around and exit, turn left to the next room. Repeat the routine. This time an old gentleman was there, seated in an easy chair with a large-print book in his lap. I glanced at the title. *Tell No One*, by Harlan Coben. Too right, I thought.

He waved me in, and I walked to the window. Bingo. I had a clear view of a slice of the street between the houses with only a few leaves in the way. As I stared across the roofs, a jogger went by. It was a neighbor from down on Brenner. So my theory was definitely possible. The bomber could have stood right where I was and watched until the Don's wheelchair rolled into view. If he was alone, no one near him, finger presses the proverbial red button and boom! Or not.

Yes, self reminded me, there were other possibilities. Like the roof. I went looking for Willard Johnson. He was in his basement cubicle and was happy to open the locked door to the roof. He enjoyed the sunshine while I crawled along the critical thirty or so feet of east-side roof edge looking for evidence of any creature larger than a Saint Bernard standing or squatting along there. Nothing, zip, nada. Okay, I thought, although it was clear from this level that it would have been ideal for the bomber's purposes. Mainly it provided a wider slice of the street in front of my home. Well, never mind. Just because I couldn't find the location where the bomber had stood didn't mean my theory was wrong. Didn't mean I was right, either.

Back downstairs I wandered the halls asking any staff I encountered if they could identify Blanche's Nurse Betty. None could, or at least they didn't. Dammit. I asked again if I could see Blanche. I was informed in blunt language that the doctor had directed she have no visitors. None. Since I wasn't family, there wasn't a lot I could do, right?

Well, I cracked the door of her room when I was upstairs and saw a nurse at her bedside. Nurse Heron, not Betty. So I left. As I reached the front door, an ambulance was just departing with an elderly resident who had suffered a fall and needed hospitalization. Lights flashing, but no siren.

With Tompkins still off the premises, I considered the possible availability of the personnel files. Nah, it was a dangerous idea. Not to mention illegal. I'd successfully burgled him once and it would be pushing my luck to try that again. Besides, Blanche's nicknames wouldn't be in those records. Then I remembered that Mr. Johnson had been here longer than almost anybody else. He was just locking up his office when I located him again.

"What? I'm on my way home an' late as it is."

"Buy you a cup of coffee?"

He chuckled. "No thanks, the stuff they have here is only good for the first hour in the morning. But now, unless they've had a run on the pot, it's heavy enough to rot your insides."

"We could go down the block. There's a coffee bar at

The Case of the Deceiving Don

Cleveland. I just have one question, really."

"Whyn't you ask it while we walk to my car?"

So I did. "I can't ask Blanche, but she mentioned a Nurse Betty, which I take it is her nickname, not her real moniker. I have a couple of questions for the nurse."

"And you don't know which one that is."

"Right. Do you?"

"Nope, can't say as I do."

"I think she smokes."

He nodded and said, "That narrows it, but there are a couple on every shift who still smoke. You know about the tree?"

By now we had left the building by a rear door and were ambling toward a dusty dark green pickup.

I said I did.

Willard squinched his face and tilted his head to stare up at the blue sky.

"Anybody you know of who's left the staff since Mr. Molinaro was killed?"

"That's two questions, and no, nobody has left."

"What about recent hires?"

We reached his truck, and Willard Johnson hopped inside and grinned down at me. "You need to talk to Alonzo. She's the last one they hired. Name's Lydia, Lydia Bettina Marie Alonzo." I think she smokes. Willard fired up the truck which belched an acrid cloud of dark exhaust and rolled out of the parking area.

Well, I thought, maybe Blanche didn't want to be bothered with all those names, so she just chose Betty. Close to Bettina. It was frustrating that I couldn't ask her directly. It was also worrisome that Blanche's health seemed to be failing.

I went back inside to look at the duty roster. Made notes as to who was and who was not on duty the day of the bombing. I wasn't sure it would help.

★ ★ ★ ★ ★

The next morning I talked with Helen Lasker. "I'm chasing a nurse at the Sheltering Limbs. My inside contact calls her Nurse Betty. It's a moniker. A nickname."

"Why?"

"She was hired after the Don showed up."

"Thin."

"I believe I have a motive pinned down." In fact, I was sure it was the right motive, but I'd learned that dealing with most cops, theories with little hard evidence usually got dismissed out of hand. Sergeant Lasker was no different.

"So tell me."

I explained my working theory that Molinaro not only smuggled drugs and other goods as well as information in and out of the prison at Allenwood, he was also running a sort of clandestine fertility clinic.

There was a pause when I finished, and then Lasker said. "And this nurse you mentioned is connected to your theory?"

"Possibly."

"And you think our dead Don substituted somebody else's sperm when it didn't take the first time, in order to keep his fee." Lasker sighed. "I'll tell you, Sean, earlier I might have laughed in your face, but I've seen a report that pretty well confirms your theory, at least the part about prisoners' sperm being smuggled out. The Department of Prisons circulates information from time to time about scams and other stuff they learn from law enforcement sources. We try to share. Anything to keep ahead of the bad guys. I have some recollection of a similar incident, maybe in California."

"Refreshing to know collective efforts are in place. Any word on Tompkins?"

"Yes, as a matter of fact. He's been detained on a federal tax-evasion warrant in Iowa. Seems the Feds took a look at the information we developed. They caught up with him in a bank in Ames, withdrawing a satchel full of cash from a deposit box there."

"Anything interesting from him?"

Lasker chuckled. "Are you serious? He lawyered up instantly."

"Do you think he had anything to do with the murder of Don Molinaro?"

"Nothing so far. I'm betting we'll discover the retirement home is a shelter for the mob and Tompkins merely a well-paid keeper. I'm of the opinion he'll turn out to be part of the unintended consequences."

"Of the bombing. Yeah, and I get a feeling Nurse Betty may be important."

"Gotta go, Sean. Stay in touch and outa trouble."

Sure, I thought, and went out into the sunny morning.

Chapter 41

I took the long way around the lake. It wasn't too warm yet, and the humidity from yesterday seemed to have gone down a little. As I stepped along the path leading out of the woods and beside the retirement home property, I spied a lone figure standing beside the smoking tree. Since I was wearing red Keds with the soft white soles, she didn't hear me approach. She was short with dark shoulder-length hair, caught in some kind of metal clasp at the back of her head. It sparkled in the sun when she bent her head to drop her cigarette butt into the can at her feet. I thought she'd start to walk away, but then she fished the pack of cigs out of her uniform pocket and lit another one.

"Good morning," I said. She started and whirled around.

"Good God," she said. "I never heard you coming."

"Sorry. I was just out for a walk."

Her smile flickered across her face and then was gone. I realized that she wasn't more'n an inch taller than me. When she raised a hand nervously to her throat, the movement lifted the hair on her neck and I saw the earring in the shape of a sparkly B. It looked as if it was fashioned of precious stones. Or really expert fakes.

"Nurse Betty," I said.

Her gaze flicked from side to side. "I'm sorry, my name is Lydia. See?" She dipped her dimpled chin and pointed to the plastic name tag on her chest.

"Yes, I do see. I also see your very nice earrings in the shape

The Case of the Deceiving Don

of a B." I smiled.

"Oh, well." She took a deep drag on her cigarette.

"For Bettina, I expect."

She nodded once and dragged the last bit of smoke out of the butt in her lips. Me and my questions were making her nervous.

"Maybe you know I've been asking around, talking to staff here."

"Yes, I've heard. What about?"

What about? Was she trying to suggest nobody in that place talked to anyone else? "You're about the only nurse I haven't talked to yet. About the bombing."

"The bombing. I see. About the Don. Don Molinaro, I guess."

Now Nurse Betty didn't seem to know what to do with her hands. She put them in her pants pockets. Then she took them out again. Her eyes skipped about like fleas trying to avoid a dog's scratching claws. She didn't look me in the eye.

"You seem nervous. I'm sorry if I'm upsetting you. But I'm at the point where I need to pin down the motive."

"The motive. You mean for the bombing? Why do you think I might know anything?"

I smiled. "Because you were not on duty that day, but you were here."

"Here?"

"Here at Sheltering Limbs. Seems odd to me that you'd be here on a day you weren't scheduled to work."

"I—well what of it? I had to get some things I forgot the day before."

"Really. Like what?"

"I don't think that's any of your business. In fact, I don't think any of this is your business. What's a dead mobster to you anyway? He was an old, worn out, nasty man. He hurt a lot of people in his time. He should have died a long time ago. I—"

her eyes widened, and she clapped a hand over her mouth. Then she whirled and ran away from me toward the back door.

I watched her go. I wondered why she was so skittish. Maybe she killed the Don. I didn't think she was a professional bomber if she had done the deed. Perhaps I'd discover that she'd been harmed in some way by Don Molinaro or one of his minions. I figured she was relatively harmless, even if she was the murderess. A calculated judgment. Even if she had bombed the old man. Greasy Gus Molinaro was old when he died. He'd undoubtedly done a lot of harm in his time. Maybe, I considered, I didn't want her to be apprehended. Maybe it was justifiable homicide. I thought these things while I walked up the street and across the front of the building to the receptionist's desk.

One of the things that sometimes happens to me when I'm on a case is that I get a feeling. I can't describe it, but it's an instinct that I'm right, or I just talked with the perpetrator. Doesn't always happen, but it's always right. I was pretty sure I had just talked to the person who blew up the Don. I didn't know why. I'd find out. At the reception desk I borrowed a telephone and called Sergeant Lasker at the Roseville PD.

"I have your bomber. If you come get her right now, I think she might tell us about it." Lasker asked where I was and said she'd dispatch a patrol car right away. There were two squads. They came fast with flashing lights but no sirens. Lasker was riding shotgun in one.

As they trooped in the door, I said to the receptionist. "We need to find Nurse Betty, aka Lydia Alonso."

"I just saw her go into the staff lounge at the end of the hall." She pointed the way. The officers' gear creaked and jangled as we walked down the long silent tiled hall. When we got to the lounge, Nurse Lydia was alone hunched over in a chair beside a table. She'd been crying. She was still crying. The sodden wad

The Case of the Deceiving Don

of tissues in one hand, and her smeared mascara were testimony to that.

She looked up at us and said. "Yes, I did it. I killed Don Molinaro."

I thought I detected a tiny bit of pride in her voice. It was obvious she was glad to confess.

Helen Lasker moved quickly to her side and Mirandized her. The other officers formed a close circle, and I stepped directly in front of her. I knew the cops were going to shut me out in a matter of moments, and I wanted some answers before that happened.

"Lydia," I said. "Why did you do it?"

"My sister was married to one of his gang. Ella wanted a baby. When Tony went to prison for life before she could get pregnant we made a deal with that—that shit—to get Tony's sperm smuggled out. I thought it was nuts, but Ella talked to me about it because I'm a nurse and she persuaded me. I gave her exact instructions. Even for one of his own family, Don Molinaro wanted five thousand dollars to get Tony's seed out. Five thousand! It was a lot of money.

"I was living in New Jersey, and I quit my job and moved to my sister's place in Pittsburgh. I found a clinic that would help us. We paid the Don, Ella got pregnant, and everything seemed fine. She had a boy and named him Tony Junior."

Lydia was standing now, her hands held by one cop behind her back. Her voice rose and her eyes blazed at me. "Everything seemed fine and then a couple of years ago Tony Junior got sick, and they did a DNA test. His father wasn't his father. We were horrified. Tony Junior got sicker and died. The doctors said if they could have found a relative, he might have been saved. We tried to find out what had happened. Nobody in town knew. Or they wouldn't tell us. By then Greasy Gus was gone. Tony died. My sister got so depressed she was hospitalized.

She's still in the hospital. I swore I'd find the Don and find out what had happened. Well, when I finally did find him, he didn't even remember Tony! And he didn't remember who had supplied the sperm he gave Ella. That man ruined my sister, my family. And he didn't care. That was when I decided to kill him. Here he was, living in this nice place with his own servant, for God's sake. And he didn't care. He didn't care about anything."

She sobbed and more tears came. She wrenched one hand away from the cop holding her and wiped her eyes.

"I read up on how to rig a small bomb. It was easy. For a while I thought I'd make it a little bomb, make him a mess, give him a lot of pain, like he messed up my family. But I couldn't figure how big or little to make the bomb. I thought I could just go away, disappear after. You know? But I couldn't." She dropped her head and sagged a little.

Sergeant Lasker put her hand on Nurse Lydia's arm. One of the uniforms put the bracelets on her wrists, and the four cops left, taking the bomber with them. I went home.

Chapter 42

Blanche Essen died that evening. Peacefully, in her sleep, just before they brought her supper. No ambulance had taken her to the hospital. There was no autopsy because the doctor happened to be at her bedside when she passed away. A few days later she was interred. Her ashes went into a bronze crypt in the ground at Golden Rest Cemetery, only a couple of miles from the retirement home where she'd spent the last few years of her life. Only Catherine and I and some cemetery workers were present.

That same day the Twins won a double-header and led their division for the first time that season. Blanche would have been pleased, although the Vikings football team was her favorite. It was sunny but not too warm, and Catherine and I repaired to a small restaurant on Larpenteur where we had an ordinary but adequate late lunch and two glasses of wine to celebrate Blanche and wish her well.

Catherine had business to attend to so I was alone at home contemplating my shaggy lawn and a woman whom I couldn't put a name to, but who appeared to be stalking me. It seemed unlikely she'd try to get to me here and now, so I pulled the ancient rotary-style lawn mower out of the shed. I grabbed the starter cord. Then caution tapped me on the shoulder, and I thought about all the ways somebody could rig the machine into a bomb. So I let go the cord handle and squatted down to examine the machine more closely. That netted me dirty hands. I couldn't see anywhere that someone had messed with the mower. It started on the second pull with exactly the kind of pops and smoke it always issued when I roused it from its slumber.

Fifteen minutes later the lawn was trimmed, I was hot and sweaty, and the only thing that disturbed my tranquil part of the universe was the distant sound of other grass cutters at work. I went for a swim. I did that quite often in the summer.

We had a nice park and beach on Lake Johanna only a mile from my house. It was usually crowded, even in the middle of a weekday, but there were no lifeguards on duty this summer because of budget cuts. A lot of people now took their kids to other, safer beaches. There used to be a big floating raft a few yards from shore, but when they took away the lifeguards, they didn't put the raft in the water.

The lake, never clear, was cool and refreshing. I'm not a strong swimmer, but I often swim in the lake for exercise. I can get in a pretty good effort in a short time. Yeah, I'm conscious of my physical health. A pot belly on a short guy like me is never attractive. Not only that, since I've hooked up with Catherine Mckerney, who is tall, slender and in excellent shape—I suspect she could bench press me—I've been even more aware. So, I did a few laps, swimming parallel to the shore from side to side among the floats that marked the limits of the swimming area.

On about the fifth or sixth lap, as I started to tire, I heard a buzzing sound that became ever louder until I could identify it as an outboard motor. I rolled over and looked across the lake toward the college campus on the opposite bank. Between us, coming through the hot spot of reflected sunlight off the water was a black shape, a boat at high speed roaring directly toward me. In my head I knew the boat would turn aside in a minute

The Case of the Deceiving Don

or two. I knew that if it hit the line of floats they would do serious damage to the prop on the motor. I knew I was far enough inside the floats that the boat couldn't reach me. I was sure of it. I thought I was.

Instinct chucked logic aside and sent me thrashing toward the beach as fast as I could manage. I didn't look back to see if the boat was gaining. That only happens in the movies. I didn't need to look. My reaching hand hit bottom and I stood up, only to lose my balance and fall to one side. That was a good thing. Over the roar of the motor, I heard two other sounds, close together. Most people wouldn't hear them. Pops, like pistol shots. I looked back to see two figures in the boat, one driving, the other appeared to be looking at me.

While I watched, seated on the sandy bottom, water up to my chin, the motor boat never slackened speed as it carved a long arc in the surface of the lake, just outside the line of floats and headed back the way it had come. Clearly, I was going to have to change my life in a big way until I caught this dolt. Whoever it was. What really bothered me was that someone knew a lot about my activities if they had a boat at the ready. Too much about my routines. I was gonna find that sucker right soon.

That evening I explained to Catherine that I would be at the office for a while. I wanted to sort through what I laughingly called my case files. I hoped to find something that would help me figure out who my stalker was. I usually made up a folder with notes and copies of bills and expenses so I had some sort of record. The operative word was usually. There were times when I did something for someone and got paid a long time later, if at all, in a free drink, or a little help with something or other, like a piece of information, or a useful contact. And yeah, once in a great while a little cash which sometimes didn't make it into my income tax statements. Things my accountant didn't want to know about, him being a bit uptight about following the tax laws. I do pay my fair share of taxes. Yes I do.

So I went to the office to paw through my old files to see if I could elicit some little clue that might help me lay hands on the stalker. My office was still not quite back to the shape I usually like it. For one thing, it was a little cleaner than usual. I'd hired a crew to come in and fix things up, repair the furniture, plaster up the bullet hole in the ceiling, clean up the blood.

Yes, there are people who specialize in such duty. Fortunately. They gave the place a serious mopping. And since I now needed new window treatments, I hired the same blind guy who had sold me the new blinds a week or so earlier. He hadn't seemed pleased to have the new business. Maybe he thought I was a blinds abuser. Or maybe he was worried he'd be the next target.

I looked through my files. I examined the ceiling. I drank a bottle of water. I doodled. Not much help. I did find a copy of a bill that had gotten misfiled and put it right. I was reaching for yet another file when I remembered something. I'd had a phone call a few days earlier from my Minneapolis detective friend, Simon. A courtesy call.

Chapter 43

I talked to Simon fairly often, but this one had been a call related to an old case. He'd informed me that the subject of that case had been paroled a week or so earlier. Elaine Higgins, that was her name. She'd murdered her drunken husband because he was basically a nasty man. He'd cheated on her and, according to neighbors, he'd frequently come home drunk and scream at her. Ultimately she cracked and one night after one of their shouting sessions, he'd fallen into an alcohol-induced stupor. Mrs. Higgins had set the bed on fire, but first she'd tied bed sheets over him so if he woke up, he'd not be able to escape.

I'd been hired by the insurance company holding the policy on the guy's life. They weren't happy with the circumstances. After some interviewing and digging around, I'd figured out that she'd probably killed the guy deliberately. Naturally, when I reported to the insurance company, they called the cops who reopened their investigation. Under state law, a miscreant can't profit from her crime. I had to testify in court. That was another case where I'd had second thoughts about the justice of it all. I mean, the guy was one nasty individual. Mrs. Higgins was a wreck, and so was her daughter. Her divorced daughter, Susan, focused on me as the reason her mother got caught. Seemed like she transferred her anger at her old man and her frustration at not being able to help her mother to me.

I'd been fortunate enough to meet the daughter only twice, and the experiences hadn't been pleasant. Understanding a little about why she was so pissed at me didn't help me tolerate the screaming. She'd hollered some very unkind things at me after I testified at trial, a trial that sent her mother to the Women's Prison at Shakopee for twelve years. With that kind of mouth, I wasn't surprised she was divorced. Elaine Higgins only served four years, being a model prisoner. I hoped the intervening time had lessened Susan's animosity toward me. The more I thought about that case, the more I wondered what was happening with her.

The next day, I decided to find out how Mrs. Higgins was doing before I looked for Susan. Maybe she'd be able to give me some insight into Susan's frame of mind. My calls to her parole officer, once I found out who that was, were not productive. Citing state law, department rules, yadda yadda yadda, he informed me at length how and why I was not to be given a telephone number, much less an address. I knew I could call in a favor and probably tease a number out of one of my telephone company contacts, but that was becoming more and more difficult to do ever since the government, in its wisdom, dismembered the big national telephone company, AT&T. There were so many companies now a self-respecting P.I. needed a telephone book to keep track.

I resorted to fundamentals and a bit of guess work. I looked up Higgins in my old Minneapolis book, the city of her residence when she'd offed her husband. There were several, and I called them, one by one.

Huzzah! On the fifth call I got surly and belligerent.
"What?"
"Excuse me, I'm trying to reach a Mrs. Higgins, Mrs. Elaine Higgins?"
"Whatchuwant?"
"Are you Mrs. Higgins?"
A pause and breathing. The voice was vaguely familiar, even

after four years. I jotted down the address and heard her set the phone down with a clunk. Then, voices in the background. A harder, wearier voice came on.

"Yes, this is Elaine Higgins, who is this please?"

"Mrs. Higgins, I'm sorry to bother you, but I was pleased to hear of your early release. I hope you are—"

"Sean!" The voice rose to a screech. "Is that you?"

I started to respond, but the woman shouted a serious obscenity at me as she dropped the phone and cut us off.

I thought about calling her back, but I suspected she'd already be calling her PO to complain about me, and I didn't need the harassment. I'd learned enough. I had an address and now knew the animosity hadn't gone away. Then I wondered if Susan Higgins McBride had learned to shoot a rifle in the intervening four years of her mother's incarceration.

I figured I'd better do one of my detecting numbers on those two. If I'd had a couple of Hamiltons in my wallet, I'd have been willing to bet one that the woman who'd picked up the phone was her daughter. So I opened my little office safe and retrieved my gat and holster. I put them into a brown paper sack and toddled off to my tired Taurus.

The Higgins place was in South Minneapolis on a quiet residential street lined with stately elms, which so far had escaped the disease practically denuding the cities of one of their principal claims to fame, a massive urban forest. The house, a clapboard two-story affair painted a faded blue, probably built in the twenties, was second from the corner. I motored past, glancing once at the numbers to verify I had the right place. Then I went around the block and parked on the cross street. A man was in the side yard on his hands and knees apparently weeding in his garden. It reminded me I needed to do the same thing. I'd been neglecting my lily patch out back.

I slid a little lower in my seat, not difficult for me, until I could just see over the steering wheel. With modern headrests, it's almost impossible to tell whether there's a driver in the car you're following down the highway, so by staying low, I'd avoid attracting attention. At least for a while. From where I sat I could see all one side of the Higgins house, the front door, and a door to the unattached garage at the back of the lot. I had no easy way of knowing if the women were in the house, but unless there was a basement door on the other side of the building, I'd be able to see anyone coming or going.

The postman went by and stuffed some mail in the Higgins' mail box. I shifted the paper bag with my rod in it away from my feet and more under my seat. I had a power bar, one bottle of tepid water, my portable battery-operated CD player, and my binocs. Hell, I was all set. Ready for Freddy. I eased the crotch of my trousers, settled a billed cap on my noggin, and cracked the off-side window. I was ready for a long watch.

Two hours dragged by during which nothing much happened. I got out my little note pad and a pen and doodled. I'd forgotten to bring any reading material. But surveillance was something I was used to. Mr. Stake-out, old Duke Farrar had once called me, because I complained less than his other operatives about such assignments. So far I was okay. No twitching curtains, no neighborhood nosy parker coming by to eyeball me. No cops.

Then one honkin' big pickup truck cruised up the street and stopped in front of Higgins' house and guess what? It was towing a boat trailer. I grabbed my small, expensive, high-powered Nikon binocs and focused. A guy got out. He looked tall—no surprise to me—and he was wearing faded tight jeans, a black muscle shirt, some kind of boots that might be cowboy boots, and an old western-style straw hat. He was clean shaven.

While I watched he sauntered up the walk onto the front

porch and appeared to knock or ring a doorbell. After a brief wait, the door opened, and there she was. My stalker. The woman I had almost decked outside my office building the night Buzz Cut got shot. Susan Higgins McBride in the living flesh. I should have recognized her that night on the street. I excused myself, reflecting that it had been four years, and her hair was different, and it was night. She wasn't holding a gun, and she looked pleased to see the dude, smiling widely in my lenses and beckoning him inside.

    I fired up the Taurus and cruised by the street where she lived, making note of the truck's license plate as I went, and headed home.

Chapter 44

The truck was registered to a Will K. Collins. He had an address in Corcoran and he was in the system in several not-so-minor ways, including simple assault and assault with a deadly weapon. He'd been clean for several years. I noodled over what to do. I finally decided the best approach was the direct. I'm that kind of guy anyway. So the next day in the morning, quite early in the morning, actually, I drove back to South Minneapolis and parked. The truck and the boat trailer were nowhere to be seen.

Good.

The sun had barely cleared the eastern horizon and a few rays shone through the mist of the morning when I leaned on Higgins' doorbell and pounded on the door itself with my gloved fist. Long ago I'd discovered two things. If you want to unsettle the target, go early and pound on the door. The cops do that. The other thing is if you pound on a door with your bare fist it hurts. So I was wearing a tan leather glove.

When I paused to take breath, I heard rattling and movement inside. The door opened a crack and I slammed my foot against the security chain. Naturally, it tore out of the wall and the door opened wide. Both women stood there, mouths open, hair tousled. In bathrobes.

Good.

"You." I snarled. I pointed at Elaine. "Do you know what your daughter has done?" I was hoping she wasn't aware that

The Case of the Deceiving Don

her daughter Susan had started a vendetta against me and that she'd enlisted the aid of her current boyfriend.

Susan backed up, and I could see the hate on her face.

I pinned her with a searing look. "If you go for the gun, if you even move, I'll put a bullet in your head." I swept my coat tail back with my right hand so they could both see the holster and the butt of my Colt semi-auto.

Elaine raised both hands to her face and then turned to her daughter. "Susan, are you messing with this guy? I told you to let it go. I don't want any more trouble!"

Susan had started to turn away and then looked back just in time to meet her mother's hand as it swept around and collided with her cheek in a startlingly loud slap. Susan's hair flew up as her head went back and she staggered. A red welt showed immediately.

I looked at Elaine and said—snarling is hard to maintain—"Either your kid or her boyfriend is a killer. She shot a guy in my office. I know they were trying for me. Never mind that he was a bad dude, but he was probably connected back East with organized crime. You better get her out of your life before somebody else shows up and I send them your way."

I stepped back, whirled around and stomped down the steps and walked rapidly to the street. My neck itched, but I felt pretty sure the rifle Susan or her buddy had been using wasn't in the house. Elaine would have freaked at that.

I could hear voices raised behind me as the two women went at it.

I fired up the Taurus and squealed out of there like I was heading for parts unknown. In fact, I tore around the block and parked again across the block where I could eyeball the place and not be seen.

An unmarked squad rolled up and paused beside me. Detective Ricardo Simon leaned out the open window and said, "You been to see her?"

"Yep. I expect her boyfriend will show up before long, and they'll run for it."

"We've checked with her PO, and she has an alibi for the murder."

"Elaine, right?"

He nodded.

"Okay. If I'm right about all this, Collins should be showing up in the next hour or so, and he and Susan will make a getaway out of town."

I was wrong by twenty minutes. Forty minutes later, Collins rolled up in his truck, eased to the curb. He beeped once, and Susan ran out of the house carrying a suitcase. She threw it into the back of the pickup and climbed into the cab.

Collins turned right at the intersection and headed toward Minnehaha. I raised an eyebrow at Detective Simon who had parked just across the street from me. He beckoned.

I went over. "Aren't you going after them?"

"Nah. We've got him covered with other cars. They'll pick him up on a routine traffic stop. I'm here to baby-sit you. We're done here so whyn't you just go home?"

I did exactly that.

Three days later, I got a call from someone in the Community Relations office of the department thanking me for my help in apprehending a pair of accused murderers. Among other weapons found when they searched Collins's truck was a rifle that ballistics demonstrated had fired the fatal shot into Buzz Cut. Susan McBride's fingerprints were all over it.

ABOUT THE AUTHOR

Before he became a mystery writer and reviewer, **Carl Brookins** was a freelance photographer, a Public Television program director and producer, and a counselor and faculty member at Metropolitan State University in Saint Paul, Minnesota. He has reviewed mystery fiction for the *Saint Paul Pioneer Press* and for *Mystery Scene Magazine*. His reviews appear on his own and other Internet sites, including *Books n' Bytes* and *The Mystery Morgue*. Brookins writes the sailing adventure series featuring Michael Tanner and Mary Whitney and the Sean Sean private detective series. He is an avid recreational sailor. With his wife and friends he has sailed in many locations across the world. He is a member of Mystery Writers of America, Sisters in Crime, and Private Eye Writers of America. He can frequently be found touring bookstores and libraries with his companions-in-crime-fiction, The Minnesota Crime Wave.